A crash from the dining room made him jump.

Lindsey came over pushing a stroller with her two little boys. She came to a surprised stop.

"Hey."

"Hey," she returned. Her curious stare made Donovan's cheeks warm. He realized he was holding the inn's account book. He fumbled for his envelope. It fluttered to the floor with other papers. "I was just slipping the rent inside," he explained. "Your aunt prefers a check."

Leo shouted, "Hey!" and Archer darted over. Donovan picked up the loose papers, and set them on the counter. The phone rang. Lindsey leaned over to get it as Leo pushed the stroller across the room and crashed it into the clock. Donovan took control of the stroller and sat on the floor to explain to the twins how the back wheels' locking mechanism worked. Archer climbed into his lap, put a thumb in his mouth and listened intently.

Lindsey hung up the phone. "I can take it from here," she said.

Donovan looked up, secretly pleased Archer had taken a shine to him. The little boy's hair smelled like bubblegum. "It's no problem," he assured her. "I'm happy to calm the chaos."

Danielle Thorne is a Southern girl who treasures home and family. Besides books, she loves travel, history, cookies and naps. She's eternally thankful for the women she calls friends. Danielle is the author of over a dozen novels with elements of romance, adventure and faith. You'll often find her in the mountains or at the beach. She currently lives south of Atlanta with her sweetheart of thirty years and two cats.

Books by Danielle Thorne

Love Inspired

His Daughter's Prayer
A Promise for His Daughter
A Home for the Twins

Visit the Author Profile page at LoveInspired.com.

A Home
for the Twins

Danielle Thorne

LOVE INSPIRED

INSPIRATIONAL ROMANCE

LOVE INSPIRED®
INSPIRATIONAL ROMANCE

Recycling programs
for this product may
not exist in your area.

ISBN-13: 978-1-335-58642-1

A Home for the Twins

Copyright © 2023 by Danielle Thorne

For questions and comments about the quality of this book, please contact us at CustomerService@Harlequin.com.

Love Inspired
22 Adelaide St. West, 41st Floor
Toronto, Ontario M5H 4E3, Canada
www.LoveInspired.com

Printed in U.S.A.

For we walk by faith, not by sight.
— *2 Corinthians* 5:7

To Declan and Nicholas—
the first stars to light the dawn of my
twilight season—for the joy you brought with
you from heaven. Thank you for choosing us.

Chapter One

Lindsey Judd's stomach did a jump, tuck and roll that made her slow the minivan to a crawl. To her relief, Kudzu Creek looked as welcoming as she remembered it. The main street still had classic Americana storefronts lining its sidewalks. Peachtree Market leaned on the corner across from the updated coffee house, and there was a new gift shop next door. A small island of grass around a flagpole marked the heart of downtown, and she turned an eager left onto her aunt's street. Pebble Stretch Road was now a curious mix of small businesses and residences, but a quarter of a mile farther, the van reached the Azalea Inn, and Lindsey crossed her fingers that the bed and breakfast would be better than she'd expected, too.

She studied her new Georgia home. In the front yard, towering twin oaks brandished fresh green leaves over the neighborhood. Their trunks were surrounded by flower-beds overflowing with fuchsia-colored azaleas. Behind them, a two-story colonial stood, flat-faced with a coat of gray paint and burgundy shutters. White hydrangeas nodded against the brick foundation of the house. "It's beautiful," Lindsey whispered in awe. A modest porch sat like a footstool at the front door, and sprawling ferns on the steps made her smile.

"What do you think," Lindsey said to the backseat. "It's not so bad." Her twin boys slumped in their car seats, exhausted after another day of fast food and travel. She turned her attention to a lovely hand-painted sign in the front yard and felt a tingle of excitement when she saw an announcement that brunches were coming soon. There was a new schedule, and she was the new chef.

"We're going to love it here," she promised her children. "It's just like home, only…" She'd visited Kudzu Creek a lot when she was younger, but she'd never seen Aunt Daphne's bed and breakfast, which she'd started with dear Uncle Jim years ago. He had passed on, and now, like Lindsey, the inn was struggling, hanging on to life by a very uncertain string. She clutched the steering wheel and took a deep breath. Together, she and the Azalea Inn were going to help each other out, because the inn needed a chef, and she needed a roof over her head.

Lindsey tugged the steering wheel and rolled into the driveway, trying to take in the vibrant landscaping without swerving onto the lawn. The blacktop ended at the back of the house and became crunching gravel. There was an outdoor firepit and a circle of Adirondack chairs off an enormous back porch, and in the opposite corner of the yard, the cottage she'd seen on the inn's website. Their new home. Could she live in such a small space with two active children for a few years? By the time the inn was firmly back on its feet, her three-year-old twins would be ready to start school, and she should have enough experience and money saved to move out. Lindsey's heart tripped a beat. Working regular office hours didn't work. Her generous parents' home was too small. The Azalea Inn was the only option.

It was a good plan.

Leo was the first of the boys to wake up

when she shut off the engine. "Mom," he grumbled, rubbing his eyes. He kicked his booster seat until it vibrated, and Lindsey hopped out. "Don't wake your brother," she shushed him. After unbuckling her oldest, Lindsey moved around to the other side of the van for Archer, while Leo gawked at the backyard. "Don't run off, Leo," she called in a loud whisper, but it was pointless, and she knew it. Settling Archer over her shoulder, Lindsey hurried to the corner of the property, pushed open the door to the cottage and gave it a sweeping examination. Archer stirred in her arms. With a curious glance at a few pieces of clothing draped over a suitcase, she laid him on a covered sofa.

"Mom!" Leo's voice sounded faint.

Lindsey glanced outside. "In here, sweetie." She walked to another promising door and found a small but full bath. There was a humble bedroom beside it that would fit the twins. She'd have to sleep on the sofa in the living room for the time being, until she figured out a better solution. She swiveled to examine the rest of the cottage. The size of the minute kitchen, if one could call it that, was alarming. It was a good thing Lindsey would do all of her cooking at the main house. She noticed a sports trophy on a dinette table beside a set of keys. *Odd.*

"Mom!" Leo interrupted in an insistent tone.

"Leo," she moaned, "what have you gotten into?" Leo planted a dirty hand on the open cottage door and gazed back innocently. He gave a small spurt with his lips, and black saliva trickled down his chin. "Stay there," she ordered and hurried to the sink. There was a sponge and new bottle of dish soap. Lindsey squirted the sponge generously, but Leo was beside her before she could turn on the tap.

"Oh, baby," she sighed, and he grinned, his smudged cheeks making him look like a chimney sweep. She crouched to his level. "You got into the firepit in the yard, didn't you?"

"I want a hot dog," Leo informed her.

"You just ate chicken nuggets a few hours ago."

"Hot dog," Leo insisted.

Lindsey sucked in a reply. Her ex insisted on having what he wanted when he wanted it, and nothing else would do. She'd admired that about him once upon a time until he'd desired a different life than she did—a new career without her or any children.

"Mommy!" Archer's sharp cry made her jump. "I'm right here," Lindsey called, feeling the familiar anxiety of being yanked in several directions. She gave up smearing ashes and soap all over Leo and stepped away from the tiny sink so Archer could see her from the sofa. "Did you wake up? Look! This is our new house," she explained.

Archer scrutinized the unfamiliar environment that looked nothing like their former home in Fort Worth and frowned.

"Hello?"

A deep voice yanked her from her sorrow, and Lindsey turned the other way. At the same time, Leo ran from the kitchen and flipped over the arm of the old sofa like a gymnast. She heard the furniture's springs crunch as the boys began to jump up and down. "Yes?"

The man who stood in the doorway didn't look like a gardener or handyman. *Bounce, bounce.* The sofa whined. Archer screeched. With shoulders broad enough to fill the entry, the handsome stranger with tawny curls and a square chin eyed her with mild dismay. "Can I help you?" he inquired. He pulled his dark green gaze from Lindsey's gaping face, and she watched his consternation turn to alarm when he noticed the streaks of soot on the walls, table and in the black, bubbling soap trail across the floor. Lindsey winced, knowing the sofa would be wet, too. "You're in my room," the stranger pointed out.

"You must be a guest." Lindsey chuckled to diffuse the situation while noting his office attire. The suitcase and trophy made sense now. She pasted a smile on her face. "This is the cottage. I live here. Your room will be in the main house."

The man stared. Archer screeched again, and Leo shouted, "*Hot* dog!" The twins began to chant their favorite menu item, and Lindsey's throat tightened with laughter. Aunt Daphne's dapper visitor did not look amused.

"There must be some kind of mistake," he replied, forcing his mouth up at the corners. He said nothing about the ashes or soap, but he looked like he was trying not to cringe at the state of the cottage.

Ignoring the children, Lindsey tucked away her amusement and strode across the room to meet him properly. "I'm Lindsey Judd," she explained, offering her hand. "I'm the new chef here, and we've just arrived."

"I see." The man gave her hand a soft shake. His eyes were soft, too, cottony, but they still looked concerned. "I'm Donovan Ainsworth, and I'm afraid I just moved in this morning. Ms. Daphne gave me the keys because we had an agreement for me to stay here." He motioned toward the key ring on the dinette table. "I just forgot to take them with me earlier."

Lindsey scrunched her forehead. "Daphne must have given you the keys by mistake," she insisted. "I'm going to live in the back of the Azalea with my boys." She motioned at her children, looking in time to see Leo help Archer straddle the piece of luggage that probably belonged to Donovan. The man gave a small gasp, and Lindsey darted over to save his jacket and tie, but she was too late. Archer had wiggled onto the top of the suitcase with the help of Leo's sticky fingers and smudged everything. Lindsey peeled the boys off one at a time. "Go sit on the sofa," she instructed them in a firm tone.

Archer gave her a petulant stare and plopped onto the floor in a pile. Leo shouted, "No, hot dogs!" and ran for the front door, slamming into the stranger on his way out. It left the side of Donovan's pants streaked with grimy bubbles. Lindsey stared in horror, but he calmly stepped over Archer to get his things. Archer started crying.

"I'll just set these outside until we get things sorted out," he said grimly.

"Hush, Archie, you're going to be okay." Lindsey felt a coil of heat unfurl from the top of her head and ooze down her neck. She hoped her embarrassment didn't show. She'd had years of experience as an office manager before the twins were born. But a full-time job and motherhood? She squeezed her fists. She could handle this.

"Archie?" Donovan picked up his dirty suitcase and headed for the door.

"Archer, actually."

He looked back at her son with curiosity, but Lindsey was used to it. She realized she was still holding the cleaning sponge and followed Donovan outside. "It's Archer. And Leo." Left alone, Archer began to howl.

Donovan set his suitcase in the grass. Lindsey felt her cheeks heat with renewed mortification when she saw soot all over it, so she bent down to wipe it off. He had to be unsettled about the cottage mix-up, not to mention his stained clothes and baggage. "You must be into constellations," he assumed in a slightly amused tone.

"Not exactly," Lindsey refuted, and he looked curious. She raised a hand. "Don't worry, we get it all the time. My husband was an astronomer."

"Oh," faltered Donovan. The sponge was smearing his suitcase. He gave her a sympathetic look instead of complaining. "I'm sorry. I didn't stop to think you might be going through a difficult time."

She gave him a faint smile, which dropped when she saw him glance at her empty ring finger. "Oh no," she said, cheeks now in flames, "I'm not widowed, unfortunately. I mean," she gasped, "not *unfortunately*. I'm divorced. My husband *is* an astronomer. My ex-husband." She looked away, unable to meet his eyes and groaned under her breath. "I meant it's just me and my boys."

"I see, and I'm still sorry," Donavan offered with sincerity. He looked rather matter-of-fact.

"I appreciate that," Lindsey admitted. "We're fine."

"Mommy!" Archer bellowed.

She sucked back a groan. "If you head up to the house, I'm sure Daphne will sort things out for you. I need to get back to Archer."

Donovan pointed across the yard. Leo had flipped a chair upside down and was using it as a ramp to launch himself into the air. "You might want to lasso that one in, too."

"Leo, do not break your legs!" Lindsey shouted in exasperation. She turned to Donovan. "You'll have more peace and quiet inside."

He gave her a sly smile that looked like a challenge. "It looks like it might be safer for your boys in there. Besides," he added with an apologetic shrug, "I've already signed a contract for the cottage, and I'm going to need it for several months—maybe as long as the rest of the year."

"The cottage was a part of my hiring package," Lindsey insisted.

The man looked put off. "You signed a contract, too?"

"Well, no." The look of mischief on Donovan's face returned. "What are you, a lawyer?" she quipped.

"As a matter of fact, I am," Donovan shot back. He grinned from ear to ear.

Dismay rippled down Lindsey's back. Of course he was a lawyer, and she was too dense not to have guessed it. Nice pants and jacket. The tie draped over the suitcase. A clean-cut look and unruffled demeanor over her claim to the cottage. She ran her fingers through her hair. "Daphne is my aunt, and I need a place to live while I help her out." Lindsey glanced back at the small little house, now dirty and bubbly inside. "I'm sorry, Donovan, but there's no way I can move us out now."

Donovan Ainsworth left his suitcase behind and walked across the lawn to the back porch while rolling up his sleeves to do battle. His parents' guesthouse was being renovated, and he needed a place to stay. The cottage at the Azalea Inn was perfect because it was within walking distance to work, and more importantly, Judge Sheldon had mentioned to him that Daphne Beasley was behind with the bank. It'd planted the idea of buying the Azalea Inn for a new charity in his head, and Donovan had let it grow. His best childhood friend, Ryan Boyington, had been gone quite a while, and it was time to make things right by honoring him. Donovan needed a home for the charitable nonprofit, and it sounded like Daphne could use an extra guest. The way he saw it, renting space in the inn while his place was under construction would give him a fly-on-the-wall's perspective into what the future might hold for the B and B, and he'd be giving them a little business while he was there.

The footsteps of Daphne's pretty niece echoed behind him, signaling she'd scooped up her children and was also on her way into the house. Undaunted, Donovan stepped through a set of French doors that led into the lounge, gave an antique mantel an appreciative glance, then continued across a plush rug to the lobby where an impressive block of reclaimed wood served as the reception counter.

Daphne was perched on a stool examining a ledger with computer printouts clipped to the top of the page. Donovan leaned against the counter and folded his arms over it. He didn't look at the numbers on her spreadsheet, but the temptation was hard to resist. "What can I help you with, Donavon?" Daphne murmured. She didn't budge at his interruption, but her round eyes shifted over her bifocal glasses.

"Sorry to break your concentration," he apologized. "I didn't get to thank you for the dish soap and other supplies. I have everything I need. It just seems there's a little mix-up over who should be in the cottage, and also, I decided to sign up for the meal plan you told me about when I checked in this morning."

Distracted from her work, Daphne flipped her glasses onto the crown of her head. "Oh,

that's right, the meal plan! Wonderful. What
do you mean mix-up?"

At that moment, Twin Number One,
who Donovan remembered was called Leo,
shouted a frustrated, "Mom!" when Lindsey came around the corner with her hand
clamped on his arm. His twin was hanging
quietly from her hip, but little Leo looked and
smelled like he'd rolled around in a campfire,
and his mother had soot smudged across the
front of her floral blouse.

Daphne forgot all about Donovan. She slid
off the stool and greeted Lindsey and her boys
with a tight hug. "Oh, look at you!" she sang.
"You made it all in one piece."

Lindsey set one twin down and let the other
go. "Yes, we all did." She glanced over her
shoulder as the boys darted off to the lounge.
"Leo, don't touch the coffee table."

Daphne waved her off. "He can't hurt
anything." A moment later, a crash from the
lounge echoed, and Lindsey gasped. "The
vase is from a yard sale, and the flowers are
fake. Don't worry," Daphne laughed. Ignoring the demolition on the other side of
the wall, she steered Lindsey by the elbow
until she stood toe-to-toe with Donovan. He
stepped back. "Donovan, this is my niece,

Lindsey. She's the new chef I was telling you about."

Daphne had told Donovan all about her, along with a meal-plan proposal. He realized after seeing the cottage's tiny kitchen, he'd need it. "Yes." He smiled. "The Texan who won't mind living upstairs."

"What?" Daphne wondered out loud. "Oh, that's right."

Lindsey made a noise of disbelief. "It seems we have a conflict of interest. I was going to live in the cottage with the boys, remember? I just went out back to see it, and it's darling, but—"

"My things are already in it," Donovan finished.

Daphne grinned at Lindsey. "Donovan called a few days ago, and I sent you an email about the changes yesterday morning."

"I haven't had time to check emails," Lindsey replied in a concerned tone.

Donovan tried not to smile. The pinch of guilt in his chest helped.

"I thought of something better," explained Daphne.

"Better?" Lindsey looked doubtful, but Donovan leaned forward with interest.

"Yes." Daphne pointed up to the ceiling. "The attic."

Lindsey's expression froze, and Donovan's pinching guilt became a stabbing sensation. He couldn't sleep at night knowing he'd relegated a small family to an attic.

"It's the master suite," Daphne beamed.

It didn't sound like much of a solution. Leo came around the corner with a bouquet of plastic flower stalks. Whatever petals had been attached were gone. He looked up at Donovan and grinned like a leprechaun. "I thought you said the suite wasn't in working order when we discussed options over the phone last week," Donovan said in confusion.

Daphne raised her chin in agreement. "The master suite had a little plumbing issue, but Bradley Ainsworth recommended a plumber, and I got it taken care of sooner than I'd planned."

"That's my cousin," Donovan announced, turning to Lindsey.

"Cousin?" Her chocolate-brown eyes looked bewildered.

"Yes, Bradley is Donovan's cousin," Daphne confirmed.

Bradley had been hired to do updates the year after Daphne's husband died, but that hadn't seemed to help business. Donovan grinned at Lindsey. She frowned, then turned to her aunt. "You want me to live upstairs in the attic, with children around your guests?"

"Oh yes, it's no trouble at all, and I think you'd like it better. We have a back staircase that leads down to the kitchen. It'd be perfect!"

A sudden cascade of thumps made them look up as Leo came sledding down the stairs on his bottom. Donovan hadn't noticed the escape artist go up, but he leaped for the last step in time to catch the child before he crash-landed on the floor. They both laughed at the same time, but Donovan's amusement faded when he saw the worry on Lindsey's face.

"People will love the twins," Daphne insisted, "and that way, I can help keep an eye on them while you're in the kitchen."

"It might work," Lindsey relented. "Having the boys underfoot in the kitchen is something I haven't had time to work out." She tossed a look at Donovan that suggested a part of her didn't want to give in. She was strong-willed, he realized, and determined, too, despite her present situation—whatever it was.

Daphne went on. "The attic takes up the

entire third floor. You'll have a bathroom and an enormous living space with a king-size bed."

"But what about reservations?" Lindsey looked genuinely concerned, and Donovan suspected that meant business was desperate indeed.

"It doesn't rent out often because of what I have to charge, and the word *attic* throws people for a loop." Daphne turned up her palms in surrender. "And it gives Donovan the quiet he needs out in the cottage."

Donovan mentally crossed his fingers. Walking in on a woman and two kids in his new place had been a surprise, but not an unpleasant one. Lindsey's doe eyes and dainty nose had made his heart stumble at first glance, and the way she patiently managed her mischievous twins was something to be admired. He didn't want her to presume he was a selfish person.

"What do you both say?" probed Daphne. She looked at Donovan.

"It's fine with me as it is," he admitted honestly. "I wouldn't mind the upstairs suite, but the cottage would be quieter for teleconferences."

Lindsey gave a slow nod of reluctant agreement. "I guess you're right," she decided, eyeing Leo at Donovan's feet. He saw the child had untied his shoelaces. With a chuckle, he leaned down to retie them, making a note to wear loafers next time he came inside.

"Come on, Leo," Lindsey said abruptly, "let's get your brother and check out the upstairs." With things settled, it seemed like she was ready to get to work, or perhaps she wanted to get as far away from Donovan as she could.

"I'll help you with your things," Donovan insisted, "since I moved my stuff in this morning before church."

She threw him another glance over her shoulder that suggested she might refuse, but Leo wrung himself from her grip and ran roaring out the back door. Archer scrambled off the couch and followed. Donovan watched an exasperated Lindsey scurry after them, trying not to laugh out loud. The woman needed help whether she knew it or not, and by the look of things, the Azalea Inn had a long way to go if it was going to save itself.

The next morning, Lindsey roused the twins to show them the back staircase to the kitchen, then seated them in front of a tiny television with their blankets. She felt guilty using children's programming for entertainment, but it would only be for an hour. Once the food was prepped, the remaining weekend guests could serve themselves at a sideboard, and she would feed the boys in the kitchen. Exploring the professional kitchen after they fell asleep the night before had been a guilty pleasure. The modernized room was outfitted with a butcher block and stainless steel counters, a six-burner gas range with a double convection oven, and an enormous built-in fridge with glass doors. There was also a walk-in pantry. Lindsey realized running her own kitchen in an inn was a dream come true, because she wouldn't have to spend years in someone else's restaurant. It made her future plans even more perfect.

"If this is breakfast, I can't wait to see what's for dinner," Daphne declared when she walked in and saw the spread ready for the dining room.

Lindsey beamed. The grits, bacon and chicken sausages were done. The eggs were about finished, and biscuits bloomed inside the oven. "You invested a lot of money into this kitchen. It's wonderful."

"The kitchen was Jim's domain." Daphne

dipped a clean spoon into the grits and tasted them. She closed her eyes in rapture. "So creamy," she sighed.

Lindsey chuckled. "Thank you. I think we have more than enough for your three guests this morning."

"Four." Daphne corrected her by raising an index finger. "I didn't include Donovan Ainsworth when you asked for numbers."

"Oh, um, right," Lindsey stammered. The convincing lawyer who'd preoccupied her mind while she unpacked in the attic last night. "I assume he'll be eating breakfast every morning?"

"Probably." Daphne planted her elbows on the counter. "Breakfasts are free, but we agreed on a long-term dining plan so he'll also have dinner options, too, now that we can offer them."

"That's marvelous." Lindsey tried to maintain some exuberance. She'd appreciated his offer to help the day before, but she'd spent so much time herding the twins, he'd ended up lugging most of their things upstairs. It was probably because he couldn't wait to get her and the boys out of his way, but at least he'd been friendly about it. "I'm looking forward to brunches, too, when you're ready to start them. It'll be fun."

Daphne's smile tightened. "We'll see how it goes. Business hasn't picked up, despite the updates I made, and the books are in the red now." She smoothed back the silver strands on her head. "You don't think this is too much for you with the twins?"

"Not if we schedule everything in advance." Lindsey's heart swirled with hope—something she hadn't felt in a long time. The twins were a handful, but she could make this work. The Azalea could be their home.

"I'm so happy you're here, Lindsey. It's been tough on me since Jim died," Aunt Daphne admitted. "I'm sorry it's because your husband wanted a different life, but the kitchen is one less thing for me to worry about, and I've missed seeing you and the babies."

Lindsey saw what she suspected was oft-disguised worry on her aunt's face. "I'm going to be fine, Aunt Daphne. My heart started healing long before the twins were born, and Keith helped me out long enough for me to get on my feet." She flipped off a blue flame on the burner and pushed a large skillet of scrambled eggs to the back of the range. "Don't worry," she added, rounding the counter between them. She gave her aunt a tight squeeze. "I know the inn is your life. You have my word I'll give the Azalea everything I have. I need a job I can juggle with the boys, and I want to be a chef more than anything else in the world. Together, we can make this place a sensation."

Daphne patted her on the back. "I sure hope so, and I look forward to you showing me how to get it all over the internet. Jim set up a website, but that was years ago."

"What we can't figure out together, we'll hire someone else to do," Lindsey assured her. The timer on her phone went off, and she hurried to the oven, pretending to ignore the fact Aunt Daphne didn't have extra money for a web designer. "Time for biscuits!" Lindsey announced.

"I better get back to the front. Save me one," Aunt Daphne pleaded. She hurried out, leaving Lindsey to do a final check on the menu and change into a clean apron. When the grandfather clock in the lobby struck six, she wiped her hands on her smock and pushed through the swinging door into the dining room with a basket of hot biscuits in one hand and a tray of bacon and sausage in the other. Two men were already seated at separate tables. Morning sunlight glimmered through the front windows, making the peachy walls glow as the coffee bar perfumed the air. *"Guten Morgen,"* said a voice behind her as she set the morning's offerings on the sideboard.

"Good morning, hello," returned Lindsey. Her first guest was lanky with a head full of white hair splayed out in all directions. She offered a hand. "Lindsey Judd."

"Karl Meyer," replied the stranger. His eyes shifted to the sideboard. "Sausages?" he asked in a German accent.

"Yes," chuckled Lindsey. "They're apple-and-chicken sausage."

He grinned back, showing a row of straight teeth. "I'm sure they'll be delicious." She handed him a clean plate from a stack of china and glanced across the room. A nice-looking man in a suit jacket turned as if feeling her notice him. It was Donovan, in full lawyerly dress. He held a cup of coffee and had a tablet set up in front of him. "Morning," he greeted her. Lindsey was surprised to feel something like dandelion seeds float across her chest when she met his gaze.

"Good morning," she returned in a steady

tone. He was freshly shaven, and as he started for the sideboard, she wondered what his aftershave smelled like. "Oh, eggs!" she blustered and spun on her heel. She hurried to the kitchen to grab the rest of breakfast, puzzling over her forgetfulness. She hadn't noticed how broad shouldered Donovan was the day before. She'd made a point not to study him too closely. Giving her head a small shake, she made sure the serving bowls had ladles and backed away with satisfaction. The other guests would be downstairs soon.

"This looks delicious," said a pleasant tenor voice. Donovan stood a step away holding an empty plate littered with biscuit crumbs.

"You didn't wait for the rest of it."

"I eat fast," he admitted. "I have to."

"Do you work here in town?"

"Yes, I have my own law office," Donovan explained."

He was a lawyer, she reminded herself, who'd easily usurped the cottage away from her. Apparently, he was successful, too. Successful, ambitious men, in her experience, had no time for anything or anyone else. "Tomorrow, it's pancakes, so you'll have to try them," she managed to say politely.

Donovan picked up a spoonful of grits and

slid them onto his plate. "Where did you learn to cook?"

"My mother and my grandfather." Lindsey felt herself soften at his sincere curiosity. "She bakes, and he could cook anything."

"Really? That's interesting."

"Yes, he was from Cuba and single for a long time before meeting my grandmother. He prided himself on his culinary skills." Lindsey arched a brow. "I bet you don't meet a lot of men like that in your line of work."

Donovan crinkled his forehead while reaching for the eggs. "What do you mean? I know lots of guys that cook."

"Do you?"

"Not exactly," he admitted.

She shrugged to make her point. "Bachelors."

A smile pulled at Donovan's cheek. "What kind of lawyer do you think I am?"

Lindsey had assumed he was a divorce lawyer. "Estate?" she fibbed.

He gave her a knowing look. "Actually I'm a personal injury lawyer, but I've done a little real estate, too."

"Oh." Lindsey fought back a guilty flush. It wasn't fair to judge him on her past experiences. "I'm sure you're good at whatever you do. What kind of real estate?"

He opened his mouth to answer but glanced over his shoulder toward the lobby and lowered his tone first. "I've helped a couple friends with closings on their properties and given some advice."

Lindsey wondered who he was afraid might overhear. "That's generous of you."

"It makes good practice, and besides, I'm looking to invest in some real estate myself soon."

"A home?" Lindsey deduced. He was staying at an inn after all, but he looked capable of buying a property for the long term.

Donovan gave a soft chuckle. "Not yet. I'd need a family for that, at least that's what my mother says, and until then she likes me nearby."

"So you're at the Azalea Inn for now."

Donovan nodded. "Our guesthouse is going through a reno, and I needed something close to work. I'm also keeping an eye out for a place to start a pet project."

"What kind of project?" probed Lindsey. Donovan pressed his lips together, and she sensed he was reluctant to share more. "It must be pretty special," she guessed. "I'm glad the Azalea Inn worked out for you."

"Me, too." Donovan's heaping plate wavered in his hands. "And no hard feelings about the cottage, I hope."

"Of course not. I should let you eat."

"Thanks. This is great, and I appreciate it." The lawyer smiled.

Lindsey couldn't help but return it. Donovan was a nice guy, despite the bad taste left in her mouth after her last run-in with lawyers, and he hadn't flinched when Leo covered him in ashes. Bonus points for that. She realized a citrusy-cedar fragrance she'd noticed wafting in the air was him. He did wear aftershave, and he smelled as good as she'd presumed. "I better go check on the boys," she stammered. "Enjoy your breakfast." Lindsey hurried back to the kitchen to pull herself together. She was only three years out of a broken marriage and one day into her new job. There would be no admiring the guests of the Azalea Inn, especially not the one who took her cottage. She had twins to raise and an inn to save.

Chapter Two

Tuesday after work, Donovan wandered up to Peachtree Market. The small grocery store on Kudzu Creek's main stretch carried fresh produce, local meat and home-canned selections along with baked goods and pantry staples. He'd no sooner stepped up to a bin of fresh bananas than he heard a sweet voice chime, "Uncle Don!"

Emily Ainsworth, his favorite almost-niece, had turned four last month, and ever since, she'd seemed all grown up. Donovan turned with a mischievous grin and stuck a banana in his ear. "Hello? Is this Claire?"

"No!" cried Emily, dashing up beside him. "It's me, not Mama!" She tugged on his pant leg until he looked down.

They both laughed, and Donovan picked

her up and held her at eye level. "What are you doing here so close to dinnertime? Did you take a nap?"

Her father, Bradley, strode up, eyes wide with exaggerated fatigue. "No, apparently we don't take naps anymore since we're almost ready for kindergarten. That means Dad's worn out by evening."

Donovan gave his cousin a quick embrace. "Was it Take Your Daughter to Work Day?"

"Emily went with me to check on an order of bricks up in Albany," Bradley explained. "Her mother needed a timeout."

"I can relate," Donovan chuckled. "I get more done working alone, too." His cousin's wife, Claire, was a ceramist and created her art in a studio behind their historical home on Maple Grove Lane.

Emily snatched the banana from Donovan and stuck it in her ear. "Hello, Uncle Don?"

"I'd like to order a pizza," he teased. She giggled, and he grinned at his cousin. Donovan gave her a little bounce. "Drop in and surprise me at work, and we'll turn on cartoons."

"Yay!" cheered Emily.

"Everyone knows you secretly watch cartoons," Bradley ribbed.

Donovan made a face of innocence. "I'm going to get all the cartoons I need at the Azalea Inn, trust me. There's only one good television, and it's in the lounge." Emily wiggled in his arms, and he set her down to examine the pile of bananas on display. "Daphne hired a new chef, and she brought along a pair of twin boys."

"Really?" Bradley inclined his head with interest. "That's good news. The updates I did must be helping business, then."

"Not that I know of," admitted Donovan. "According to Judge Sheldon, the bank issued a foreclosure warning. I think a chef is a last-ditch attempt to save the place."

"And you think it will close?"

"I don't know, but once I finish the paperwork to set up the charity, I'll need to decide on a property. Between your updates and Lindsey's breakfast this morning, I'm not sure the Azalea Inn is ready to surrender, but I like the look of it."

"Lindsey?"

"Lindsey Judd. She's the chef," Donovan explained.

"What's her husband do" joked Bradley. "Dishes?"

"There is no husband. Apparently, he bailed some time back."

"With twin boys?"

Donovan raised his chin in agreement at his cousin's tone. "I think they're about three years old. Not everyone's ready for that."

Bradley looked at his daughter with affection. "Where are they living?"

Donavon told him about the misunderstanding with the cottage rental, then shared the details of Leo's exploration into the firepit. Bradley laughed. "It sounds like Emily may have some new friends soon. Did you tell their mother the park is almost finished?"

"That's right," Donovan said, remembering the new playground. "No, I didn't. You did a fantastic job renovating the schoolhouse museum. How long before the playground is done?"

"I hope before the end of the summer," his cousin guessed. "It was supposed to be done last spring, but…"

"Scheduling, I get it." Donovan twisted his lips. "Trust me. I'm in a little cottage now because of it."

"Yes, I'm sorry about that," apologized Bradley. "Too bad I'm not doing things myself there."

Donovan patted him on the shoulder. "Just get me out before I starve to death," he begged. "Mom is texting me every night to see if I've eaten."

"Staying at the Azalea Inn with a chef on hand sounds like a good deal."

Donovan caught himself matching his cousin's gaze for a second too long. He shifted and picked up a few bananas to juggle for Emily's entertainment.

"What?" wondered Bradley.

"What?" repeated Donovan, juggling furiously.

"You look funny."

"This is my normal look."

Bradley laughed, then took Emily by the hand before she started tossing bananas around to mimic Donovan. "Is the new chef interesting to you or is she just a good cook?"

One of the bananas plopped to the floor. Donovan looked around to make sure the store owner, Mr. Hughes, had not spotted him. "She's both," he said, trying to sound nonchalant. With her peaches-and-cream complexion, the truth was Lindsey was more than interesting; she was attractive to him. It was a tempting combination at first glance. She certainly had it together, and he found that admirable, too. He leaned over with a groan and picked up the dropped fruit. "It's not a big deal."

"Are you sure?" Bradley's tone had a teasing edge.

Donovan gave him a solid nod of affirmation. "I'm not looking for a ready-made family." He felt his cheeks warm, hoping he hadn't crossed a line. Bradley had married Claire over a year ago. She'd had custody of his daughter, Emily, and Bradley's adventurous forage into fatherhood and eventual wedded bliss had been bittersweet for Donovan to watch. "I mean, I never thought about it," Donovan amended. The truth was, he was more than ready to find the one God had saved for him all these years—he'd planned to marry right after law school, but it hadn't worked out. But a ready-made family? No. The law degree, yes. A law office in his hometown, absolutely. And with Ryan's charity just getting underway, he could check that off his list soon, too. But a woman with kids had never been a goal.

"It's okay. I understand," said Bradley. He scooped up Emily with a free arm. "But just remember, God doesn't always have the same objectives we do." Donovan nodded. He was sure God had something in mind for him other than someone else's twin boys.

"Right, enjoy your bananas then." His cousin smiled. "It looks like we're having peanut-butter-and-banana sandwiches tonight."

"Yum," mused Donovan agreeably.

"Bye-bye, Uncle Don." Emily waved.

Donovan blew her a kiss as she disappeared with her dad and their groceries. His stomach rumbled. He chewed his lip wondering if his mother would mind if he showed up at her house, because for some reason, all of Bradley's questions about Lindsey had made him uncomfortable. He wasn't sure he wanted to hurry back to the inn for dinner, even though he'd bought the meal plan. Donovan grabbed the three bananas he'd touched. After visiting the café again, he could take them home as snacks—or bribes—in case he came across two little monkeys.

Lindsey spent her first week at the inn setting up the master suite. She made a toy box for the twins and tucked in puzzles, play-sized cooking utensils and spongy balls that wouldn't do any damage if they were thrown at a fragile target. The suite had a bed and a large couch that pulled out. She took the bed for herself, knowing the twins would eventually join her on most nights. She'd worry about a trundle later. After playtime in the yard, Leo and Archer fell asleep as she read them books, so she turned on a baby monitor and snuck out to prepare dinner.

A charming antique mirror in the lobby had been turned into a chalkboard to announce evening meals, and Lindsey carefully wrote out the menu. Since it was her first weekend, she whipped up a marinade and pulled out her best peach cobbler recipe. By the time the cobbler was cooling and vegetables prepped, the twins were muttering on the baby monitor. She covered everything up to keep it fresh and tiptoed up the stairs to surprise them. They did laundry together in the inn's fusty basement, and then to her delight, Aunt Daphne offered to take the boys on a walk to meet her friend Diane.

"That would be helpful," Lindsay said with gratitude. "I bet they would like to see their new neighborhood, but I recommend doing it with a stroller to keep them contained."

Aunt Daphne laughed in a rich, musical tone. She'd just signed in a couple from Chattanooga on their way to the Florida panhandle. "I don't think I could wrangle them without one. And by the way, Mr. and Mrs. Franklin are excited to have a home-cooked feast."

"No pressure," Lindsey joked, while Leo shouted, "Walk!" and Archer joined him in the demanding cheer. Her mind spun with so many dinner details, she almost missed their attempt to boost each other up onto the lobby counter. "Oh no, you two," she warned, "Aunt Daphne went to get your stroller."

"We walk!" Leo announced. Lindsey herded them out to the front sidewalk and waved her aunt off. Within the hour, the food for the evening's supper was almost ready, and the boys and their great-aunt had returned. Lindsey took the twins upstairs, and once they were surrounded with toys and an alphabet video on her tablet, she hurried down to finish up meal preparations. She had just plated a fruit salad when someone rapped on the swinging door to the dining room.

"Coming!" She snatched up two bowls of pretty fruit drizzled with light-tasting lemon sauce, but the door pushed open, and Donovan Ainsworth stuck in his head. She glanced sideways at the oven clock. Donovan had only showed up to eat once so far and disappeared quickly afterward. "Hello, there," she greeted him. "You're in time for dinner. The first course is on its way out."

"First course?" He ran a hand down the back of his neck in a way she found strangely alluring. "I was just hoping for a plate of something hot. I've eaten takeout the past few days and can't bear it again."

She smiled and held up the bowls of fruit. "Tonight's a special occasion since it's the end of my first week."

"Then I better have a seat." He smiled with anticipation. "There's a couple in here, too, by the way, and I'm sure the rest will be down shortly unless they don't like the smell of pot roast."

Lindsey breezed past him. "It's prime rib, actually." He reached over her with a long arm to prop open the door, and she ducked underneath catching a whiff of his fruity-cedar scent. She arranged a welcoming look on her face and served the couple from Tennessee first. Donovan chose a seat behind her, and she hurried back to grab his fruit wondering how someone could smell so divine. "How was your walk to work from the cottage this week?" she asked when she returned to the dining room.

"Great. It's nice to stroll downtown in the quiet before the sun rises." Donovan stuck a spoonful of melons and strawberries into his mouth.

"Then, you must leave before the twins wake up, because it isn't quiet after that." In fact, it took everything Lindsey could think of to keep them from running back and forth across the floor. She'd finally decided to let them jump on the bed until the rest of the house began to stir. "Enjoy your meal." She realized as she hurried into the kitchen to slice the meat that she was starved for adult conversation. Lately she was talking Aunt Daphne's ear off every time she caught her at the front register, and now she was chattering to the guests while they ate. Rueful, Lindsey toted everyone's plates out to the dining room on a large service tray.

Donovan pretended to faint with delight when he saw the prime rib, and she caught herself smiling when she returned to the kitchen to deposit the fruit bowls into the sink. With a modest eye roll at his praise, she went in search of ice cream. Despite the fact that Donovan was living in the cottage she'd wanted for herself, she found him kind, responsible and even funny. She couldn't help but admire him although he was ambitious, but he was also practical and fair—not unlike someone she'd once loved. Lindsey pursed her lips as she scooped steaming peach cobbler onto a dessert plate. Being practical and fair wasn't always a selfless thing. Her heart dropped into a little puddle of resentment that hadn't completely dried up in her soul. People could act practical and still be cold and selfish, too. As if in agreement, the frozen ice cream put up a fight while she attempted to scoop it out to accompany the cobbler.

"That was the best meal I've had in weeks." Donovan's voice echoed through the kitchen after dinner, just as Lindsey dipped her hands into a sink of soapy water. She looked over her shoulder in surprise. "You didn't have to bring in your dishes. I would have come out for them."

He carried his plate and bowl inside anyway and set them on the counter. "I really don't mind, and like I said, I appreciate the meal."

A smile tweaked Lindsey's cheek. "That much is true."

"Besides," Donovan continued, "we might as well work together while we're here. I'll look out for the boys if they get outside, and you can swap me with breakfast in the mornings." He wrench his lips suddenly as if worried about something. "Although Southern Fried Kudzu is going to think I've been kidnapped."

"Southern Fried Kudzu?"

"It's the café downtown. They make great tarts. Homemade."

"I'll check them out, and you have yourself a deal," agreed Lindsey. "I don't let the boys go outside by themselves, so if you ever see them out back, I'd appreciate it if you'd let me know."

"Sure thing."

Standing so near to him, Lindsey realized Donovan was a head taller. His warm gaze flitted past her, and she studied his square jaw. He was different. He made her feel something she hadn't felt in a long time.

"I guess I should let you know…" he said in a low tone as if reading her mind.

"What?" Lindsey blinked, suddenly vulnerable. Donovan pointed past her. She swung her gaze to the door that led out to the back porch. Through the screen, she saw Leo with one leg over the handrail and Archer crouched in a ball so his brother could use him as a step stool. She gasped and shook

the water off her hands. "Boys!" she cried
in alarm. The swinging door to the kitchen
burst open, and the wife of the couple she'd
served stepped in.

"Ms. Judd?"

"Yes? I—" Lindsey felt breathless as she
tried to compose herself.

"Could I get that cobbler recipe?" Mrs.
Franklin began, "It's wonderful—"

"Ah-ha!"

Lindsey pivoted at the sound of Leo's tri-
umphant cry. He was standing on the top of
the porch railing with one foot in front of
the other like a tightrope walker. "Leo!" she
called out, forgetting about her customer.

"Oh my," gulped the woman.

Lindsey didn't wait for any more compli-
ments. She dashed out the door. Snatching
Leo by the waist, she set him firmly onto the
ground and gave Archer a menacing frown.
"Stop helping Leo climb things. He's going
to get hurt!"

Archer nodded like a sage. "He fall down."

Behind her, Donovan cleared his throat.
"Would you like me to watch them for a moment?"

Lindsey looked back without trying to
hide her exasperation. "Just for a minute.

Yes, please." She felt her nerves tangling. She'd raised the boys three years with little assistance, outside of her parents', but keeping control of them while running a bed-and-breakfast's kitchen was going to be a challenge. She was going to need help, she admitted, but going to Keith was no longer an option.

She marched back into the dining room. The Tennessee couple was bidding Daphne farewell as if they had plans to walk into town. Daphne handed them a printed flyer listing all of the enchanting shops on Creek Street that Lindsey hadn't had the chance to visit. She couldn't ask her aunt to watch the boys any more than she already did—the woman was trying to save her own hide.

Lindsey's brain flitted back to Donovan with a little encouragement from her unsteady pulse. The lawyer? As achingly handsome as she found him, he had his own career and a life that didn't include children, and besides, she hardly knew him. He was certainly no babysitter. Lindsey's heart pinched with distress, but she shook off the doom and gloom. "Excuse me?" she called out to the guests, "You were wanting my recipe?"

Aunt Daphne beamed when Mrs. Franklin

said with enthusiasm, "Yes, if you wouldn't mind." She dug through her purse for a pen and paper, and Lindsey generously recited the recipe from memory as they stood together on the front steps. Afterward, feeling buoyed, Lindsey returned to the kitchen to save Donovan. But the room was empty.

Hurrying to the back porch, Lindsey scanned the yard and saw a dress shirt lying in the grass. There was a broomstick in the firepit. She gazed heavenward and groaned. After striding down the stairs, she headed for the cottage. The door hung open. It looked like the boys had dragged some of Donovan's belongings into the yard. She cringed. No matter how nice the man was, he hadn't signed up for this. Why stay at the Azalea Inn long term anyway? she wondered. It had to be more expensive than other options.

She stopped at the threshold of the cottage door in surprise. Donovan was crouched on the floor with a broken sports trophy. Leo and Archer were exchanging handfuls of protein bars and snack-sized bags of beef jerky in the tiny kitchen. "Excuse me, have they—"

Donovan looked up with a pale face.

"Oh, boys!" scolded Lindsey, "get out of Mr. Donovan's snacks." She hurried to help pick up pieces of the broken trophy. There were remains of a track-and-field hurdle and pieces of the torso of a runner scattered across the floor. Donovan clutched the base and two shimmery red strips in one hand. A brassy knob was in his other.

She groaned and crouched down beside him. "Did the boys do this? I'm so sorry." Lindsey glanced at a name plaque lying on the floor beside his feet. *Ryan-somebody,* it said. "Can I—" She scrambled around to pick up more pieces as Donovan composed himself, hiding the disappointment she'd already detected. "I'm mortified," Lindsey apologized.

"It's fine, it was just on the table, I mean—" He didn't sound fine.

She peeked at him, sick at heart that the twins had broken something so personal. "Leo, Archer," she commanded in a firm tone, "tell Mr. Donovan you're sorry and go outside. Now." She pointed for emphasis. The boys looked slightly confused, then hurt. Archer began to bawl. Leo dashed for the door with a chocolate protein bar gripped in his hand.

She reached out to catch him and missed, but Donovan said, "No, let him go. It's okay."

Embarrassed, Lindsey held out pieces of the trophy, and Donovan set the base down and cupped his palms. She sprinkled them into his hands and met his deep green eyes with regret. "That was obviously important to you," she choked. "I can glue this back together. It's no problem."

"No," he refused, trying to smile. "I can do it later."

She cringed. She'd hoped he would say it wasn't important or that it was just a tacky old trophy, but it clearly meant a lot. "Let me know if you need any help," she insisted. He gave a swift jerk of his chin, then carefully arranged the broken pieces on the coffee table. "You must have run track," Lindsey guessed.

Donovan glanced past her, and she looked outside to make sure Leo wasn't in the firepit again. "Yes." His reflective tone brought her back, but he was lost in a memory. "My best friend and I did. We ran until our senior years."

She slanted her head. "Why did you give it up?"

"No, I ran my senior year, I meant. Ryan... He, uh, he quit school."

"Oh." Lindsey tried to act like she understood, but she didn't. Why would Donovan keep someone else's trophy? She touched him on the elbow, grateful he didn't flinch. At least he wasn't angry. "I'm truly sorry," she said again. "I'd be happy to replace it."

"No, it's fine. Some things can't be saved." He exhaled. "I shouldn't have brought it along. It's just…" When he trailed off, she waited. It was usual to see Donovan Ainsworth with something heavy on his mind. He blinked, then came back to her. "Yeah, he, um…" Donovan hesitated again. "He was like a brother to me, and he died a few years ago."

"I see," said Lindsey. Perhaps Aunt Daphne had known Ryan. She'd have to ask.

"Mama," interrupted a little voice. Lindsey looked down. Archer stood at her feet with a chewed piece of plastic. He held it up in frustration, and she saw it was a stick of beef jerky. "Open, please."

She glanced at Donovan, and he nodded his permission. "Archer," she breathed, grateful for the distraction. She crouched down and ripped the beef jerky open for him. "I guess I should have fed you before dinner service," she sighed. She climbed to her feet, swinging Archer up onto her hip. "Thanks for the help back there. I'm really sorry about the trophy."

Donovan waved her off. "I'll keep the

door locked in the future. It's not something I thought about before. Kudzu Creek is a safe town, but I didn't think about the kids."

Lindsey nodded like she understood, but the awkwardness felt terrible. "Well, if there's anything else I can do, let me know."

Donovan didn't answer, so she hurried out feeling his gaze on her back. When she heard the sound of the cottage door click shut, something fizzy skipped down her spine. He was an interesting man. He'd sparked long-dormant feelings in her in the kitchen, had patience with her twins and held the tender memories of his friends sacred. Lindsey exhaled and tossed her head to clear her admiring thoughts. Donovan may have treated her and the boys kindly, but he was clearly not interested in a family to go along with his successful career and ambitious goals. Besides, he had a lot going on in that head of his that did not include romancing a chef.

Chapter Three

Donovan tried to ignore the broken trophy pieces all over the coffee table. He went to church with his parents on Sunday, ate dinner at their house afterward, and only casually mentioned the Azalea Inn's new chef during the dinner conversation—but he couldn't help sharing humorous stories about the twins' antics at the inn. An orange sunrise crept over the rooftops of Kudzu Creek as he walked to work. He knew the curious boys hadn't meant to break the trophy and wasn't really upset. It'd just been an unexpected disappointment. The children were a part of the Azalea Inn, and as perplexing as it was, he didn't mind them—or their mother. The problem was the location—both house and cottage—were perfect for his halfway house where young men would stay after completing a drug recovery program, and now he was sure he wanted it.

Donovan's musings scooted to the back of his mind when he spotted Judge Sheldon strolling back and forth in front of the office with his copper-red dachshund, Kessler, on a leash. "Hello, Judge," Donovan called, wondering if he'd forgotten a promise to walk his favorite pup for his friend. He'd been walking the judge's dogs ever since he was a teenager and needed a part-time job. These days it was for relaxation and fun.

Judge Sheldon raised a hand in greeting. His usual round glasses were perched on the tip of his nose. Donovan unlocked the door and welcomed him inside. "Did Kessler and I have an appointment?"

"No. I thought you might be along soon and needed to stretch my legs. How are things at the inn?" Judge Sheldon asked.

Donovan tapped on the air conditioner and motioned toward the lobby's couch. He dropped onto it and sat back, crossing one ankle over a knee. The judge eased down beside him and commanded his wiry pet to lie down at their feet. Donovan leaned forward and scratched Kessler around the neck. "Better than expected."

Judge Sheldon guffawed. "I would expect so with free meals and the lovely Daphne Beasley waiting on you."

"Breakfast, yes, and they've started offering dinner, too," Donovan acknowledged. "You should come by."

The judge raised his white eyebrows. "I take that to mean things are improving."

"It looks like they are," Donovan admitted. "Between me renting out the cottage and the new chef, the inn doesn't appear to be leaking money as badly, but I know those renovations a while back came with a hefty price tag, and like you said, she's behind in her bank payments."

Judge Sheldon made a soft noise in his throat. "It's good of you to help Daphne in her last attempt to stay afloat by renting the cottage." He scanned the reception area that Bradley's wife, Claire, had decorated with refinished antiques and her own stunning pottery.

Donovan shrugged. "I assume if things don't pick up faster, she'll have to throw in the towel."

"I think your idea to open a halfway house in its place is a wonderful idea," the judge told him.

"The residents could easily get jobs at Southern Fried Kudzu or the Peach Market, and they could walk to work," Donovan explained with growing enthusiasm.

Judge Sheldon added, "There's also counseling at the social services office around the corner from the church." .

"These will be good boys," Donovan promised. "Local young men who've battled addiction and want to change." *It was too late for Ryan.*

"Your heart is in the right place."

Donovan smiled modestly.

The old fellow chuckled, but then it faded off. "Speaking of that, Ainsworth, I have to confess I have an ulterior motive for stopping by."

"What can I do for you?" Donovan straightened with interest.

"It's my grandson," admitted Judge Sheldon. "He's gotten himself into a bit of trouble and needs some community service hours. I know there're many programs to choose from, but I was wondering if he could do something for you." The judge gave a pained smile. "I thought if Isaac could see the aftermath of what texting and driving can do, firsthand, he might take adulting a little more seriously."

Donovan vaguely remembered that charges had been pressed against the judge's grandson a few months ago. "Reckless driving isn't a joke, that's for sure." He raised his gaze to the ceiling and thought. "I'll tell you what, give me a few days, and I'll get back to you. I don't need anyone in the office right now, and I already have an intern that takes photographs at accident scenes and the impound lot."

"I appreciate it," said the judge. "He's good with computers and technology, obviously."

Donovan offered a hand. "I don't mind at all."

Judge Sheldon shook it, then shortened Kessler's leash in his hand. "The Azalea will be a good option for your project, if it works out. I'll see you later. Are you going to be at Southern Fried Kudzu this week?"

Donovan grinned. "I just texted Bradley to meet me there for lunch."

The older man exhaled in a long stream. "You know it's my favorite place to eat, but it's killing my cholesterol levels. I need to find another spot to loiter."

"Why don't you join us anyway," Donovan suggested. "A little fried kudzu can't hurt."

* * *

After breakfast service ended the next morning, Lindsey picked up a tray of eggs while giving Donovan a sideways glance. He'd pushed his half-empty plate aside and was scribbling on a legal pad. She wondered if it was for a case.

"Lindsey?" Aunt Daphne drew her attention to the foyer with a breathless voice.

"Is everything okay?"

"Yes," her aunt assured her. "It's just I had a phone call." Her eyes glimmered with enthusiasm.

"It must be good."

Aunt Daphne glanced around the dining room. Mr. Meyer had left, as well as the couple from Tennessee, and they'd only had two new reservations, not counting Donovan in the cottage. "Do we have more eggs?"

"We have plenty." Lindsey made sure the kitchen stayed stocked.

Daphne exhaled. "Good. Then, expect four more for breakfast in about fifteen minutes."

Lindsey glanced toward the stairs. The twins had been alone upstairs for half an hour but all seemed quiet on the baby monitor in the kitchen. "I'll go check on the boys," Aunt Daphne offered.

"Okay." Lindsey took a deep breath. "Unexpected guests?"

"Not exactly," Aunt Daphne explained. "My friend Diane called. She owns Alabaster's, the adorable little gift shop in town." Lindsey slanted her head in curiosity. "I know you haven't been there, so we'll have to visit sometime," Aunt Daphne promised. "She's bringing a few friends with her to breakfast today. I told her we're opening up the dining room to the public, and she wanted to help spread the word."

"That's kind of her."

"It is," agreed Aunt Daphne. "I know it's a bit of a late notice, but I didn't think you'd mind. I'll get the boys."

Lindsey gave her a crisp nod. Turning to the kitchen, she saw Donovan climb up from his seat and put on his blazer. She picked up an empty water pitcher and approached him to wish him a good day. "How was breakfast?"

"Good as always." He glanced back at the sideboard. "You make wonderful blueberry muffins, by the way."

"Thanks. It's the splash of lemon juice and tiny pinch of ginger." Lindsey noticed he'd scribbled *Taxes on charitable contributions* across the top of his legal pad. He saw her looking, and she flushed. "Charity aid?"

"Something like that," he answered with an air of mystery. "I'd ask you how business is coming along but—"

"Don-o-van!" A woman trilled his name from across the room.

Lindsey swung her attention to the lobby in surprise. There were four ladies, three of them old enough to be her mother, gazing at Donovan with adoring glances. "I think it's your fan club," she whispered, trying not to laugh.

One of them slid between the tables with her arms outspread, a silver bob swinging side to side at her chin. "I hoped I'd catch you here."

"Mom?"

Lindsey felt her eyes widen with interest. She told herself she should return to the kitchen, but she couldn't resist seeing Donovan caught off guard, and by his mother, of all people.

"I wanted to surprise you," beamed the woman.

"You certainly did."

Lindsey watched Donovan's cheeks become cherry red and found it so endearing she had to bite back a smile. She waited to be noticed, and it only took his mother about three seconds to grant her wish. "Oh, are you…?" The lady looked back and forth between Lindsey and Donovan, then down at Lindsey's apron.

"I'm the new chef of the Azalea Inn," Lindsey explained.

"Is that so?" The woman leaned forward on the toes of her white tennis shoes. "I thought you might be a 'friend.'" She made air quotes with her fingers.

Donovan coughed. "She is a friend, Mom, and I need to get to work."

The woman pouted. "I wanted to see your cottage. At least introduce me."

"Lindsey, this is my mother, Viola. Mom, this is Lindsey. She's from Texas."

"Call me Vi," Viola instructed Lindsey. "I understand from your aunt that you have two little boys."

"Yes," Lindsey conceded when Vi didn't miss a beat. "Aunt Daphne is checking on them now."

"Oh, that's where she went." Vi looked back to the lobby and waved her friends over. "Come meet Lindsey, girls," she insisted.

The group came over and greeted Donovan, and he gave each one a quick hug. "I should get to work," he announced. "Claire, would you remind Bradley we have a lunch appointment tomorrow?"

"You mean a play date? Yes, of course," a petite blonde teased him.

Donovan glanced at Lindsey. "This is Claire, my cousin Bradley's wife, and Ms. Olivia, who lives across the street from her on Maple Grove Lane."

"Hello," said the antique Ms. Olivia, who Lindsey realized was wearing a wig. The remaining guest, a woman with short, silvery-white hair waved in greeting. "I'm Diane. I've known your aunt for years."

Lindsey held out her hand. "She's told me about your shop. It's nice to meet you." Lindsey realized Donovan was watching her. She sent him a bemused smile. "I better run," he said and rushed for the door.

"Donovan, you call me," his mother called with none of her sugary Southern accent.

Lindsey almost laughed because the tone sounded just like hers when she scolded the twins. She took a deep breath. "Ladies, there is a buffet on the sideboard with all of the dishes and silverware you need. Just help yourselves." She turned to escape, but Vi called her back.

"Oh no, you can't run off now. You have to join us."

Lindsey tensed. "I shouldn't," she protested. "Let me fetch more muffins." She hurried to the kitchen. It wouldn't be professional to sit with customers while they chatted and ate, but maybe that was acceptable in a place like Kudzu Creek. Aunt Daphne probably would have accepted the invitation. The women had filled their plates when Lindsey returned—all but one. Claire Ainsworth was hovering around the buffet, fluffing a napkin in her hand. She looked up and offered Lindsey a pert smile. "Is everything okay?" Lindsey asked.

"It looks wonderful."

"What else can I get you?"

"Besides eggs, ham, fruit and these lovely muffins? Nothing," laughed Claire. "I just wanted to meet you good and proper. Donovan's told me a little about you."

"He has?"

"Yes," Claire admitted. "At dinner at his parents' home last Sunday. I'm married to his cousin, Bradley."

Lindsey recognized Donovan's cousin's name. "I believe he's mentioned him."

"I'm not surprised." Claire picked up a napkin. "They're practically inseparable. I just wanted to say hello. I understand you have children close to my daughter's age."

Lindsey shifted her feet with interest. "You have a daughter?"

"Yes, Emily. She's four. Donovan didn't tell you about her?"

"No, I don't think so."

"Well," mused Claire, "he babysits for us sometimes, and he's her favorite pet so I'm sure he's enjoying having your boys around."

Lindsey reared back in surprise. "He babysits?"

Claire chuckled. "Yes, he's really good with kids although he doesn't think so."

Lindsey realized she *could* believe this.

"You have to see him in action," Claire explained. "Sometimes he takes off the suit."

"I have," admitted Lindsey. "He's very patient."

Lindsey wondered if Claire knew the boys had broken Donovan's trophy. "Here," she insisted, "let me help." She took Claire's teacup and escorted her to the table where the other women were eating. Diane held out a chair, and Vi pulled another one away for Lindsey. "Please do sit down, Lindsey, just for a moment," pleaded Vi.

Lindsey glanced toward the stairs. She didn't want to disappoint Donovan's mother. She seemed sincere. "Just for a minute? I want you to enjoy your time here."

"Oh, we will," exclaimed Diane. Beside her, Ms. Olivia took small, determined bites from her plate, like a little bird.

"How are you liking Kudzu Creek?" questioned Vi, then she added, "Is my son behaving himself?"

For some reason, Lindsey flushed. "He's no trouble at all, and he's even helped with the boys a few times."

"That's good to hear," Vi said.

"He's a handsome boy," Ms. Olivia chimed in. "Isn't he handsome?" She turned to Claire.

"I suppose." Claire chuckled. "Although I prefer his cousin."

Diane laughed. "And Donovan prefers his office, doesn't he?" She winked at Lindsey. "Does he work during breakfast all the time? I saw his tablet out."

"No," Lindsey replied then wondered if it'd been a tool to avoid her. "Just lately." As if sensing her unease, the ladies quieted. "I think he has a lot on his mind," she explained.

"He works too much," sighed his mother. "He always has."

Diane chimed in. "He's always going a hundred miles an hour. High achiever."

"Lists and goals and schedules," his mother continued. "That's why I encouraged him to move near us," she explained. "We have a guesthouse on our property, and that's where he stays so I can make sure he eats and sleeps."

"Until you gave him the boot," Ms. Olivia pointed out, "and high time."

Claire burst into laughter over her muffin. Diane waved her hands around like batons. "Oh, come now, Ms. Olivia. He could live somewhere else if he wanted, but why move into a house all alone when his mama has plenty of room?"

"We're remodeling," Vi explained to Lindsey.

"Yes, he told me," Lindsey assured her.

Vi didn't even take a breath before continuing, "Where did you move from, Lindsey?"

Lindsey tried not to exhale with relief that the topic of Donovan living at the inn had changed direction. "Fort Worth."

"And you have two children?"

Vi certainly liked to have her facts straight. Lindsey could see questions in everyone's eyes and decided to tackle them before they got the wrong idea. "I was married almost two years," she explained. "My husband changed his mind about having a family after he was promoted at NASA, but the boys were already on their way."

There was a moment of silence. "I'm so sorry," said Vi, as if suddenly remorseful she'd asked so many questions. Claire gave Lindsey a sympathetic look.

"So you came to Kudzu Creek to live with your aunt," concluded Diane.

"To *work* for her," said Lindsey quickly. "My parents helped me out for a while, but it was time to move forward."

"How long have you been a chef?" Sweet Claire seemed determined to keep things light.

"I graduated from culinary school before I got married," Lindsey said, "but I became an office manager because the hours worked better for my husband. He was getting his PhD."

"He's a doctor?" asked Ms. Olivia.

"His doctorate, Ms. Olivia," repeated Diane in a loud voice from across the table. "A degree."

"Oh. I need another muffin," Ms. Olivia grumbled.

Claire jumped up before Lindsey could. "I'll get it. I want one, too."

"I should get back to the kitchen," Lindsey confessed. "It was nice to meet all of you."

"It was nice to meet you, too," Vi replied. "I couldn't get a word out of Donovan. No details anyway." She shrugged. "Boys. So we decided to make a breakfast date."

Lindsey smiled. "I know Aunt Daphne appreciates your business."

"It's quite lovely here," sighed Diane. "You should come downtown and visit my shop, Alabaster's. We squeeze in a book club there once a month. Do you like to read?"

"I love to read," said Lindsey. She got to her feet as the outdated telephone jangled from the lobby counter. "When I have the time."

"You must come," Vi declared.

Claire brought the muffin basket to the table. "Do you mind?"

"Not at all," Lindsey assured her. Instead of leftovers, she could feed the twins peanut butter and jelly on toasted bread.

"Let's have the book club here," squawked Ms. Olivia as she stole another muffin from the basket.

Lindsey blinked as the prospect raced through her mind. "We certainly have the room."

"That's not a bad idea," mused Diane.

Donovan's mother snapped her gaze back to Lindsey. "Aren't you going to start having brunches soon?"

"Yes, by reservation. We just haven't started."

Vi grinned like a Cheshire cat. Lindsey realized Donovan had her eyes. "And here we've been worrying about the Azalea Inn and what we can do to help." Vi dipped her chin at Diane. "The Kudzu Creek Book Club can move from the back room of Alabaster's Gifts to the Azalea Inn."

"Sounds good to me." Claire beamed.

"Sounds delicious to me," Ms. Olivia chimed in. She gave Lindsey a glowing smile before stuffing the remaining half of a blueberry muffin into her mouth.

Chapter Four

A week later, Donovan dashed through the lobby of the inn to drop off his payment for the next month. There was no one at the front desk. He tried a drawer and found it locked. He noticed Daphne's green account book stacked beneath a pile of welcome packets and looked around. He'd hoped to talk to her about the judge's grandson again. He'd mentioned to her Isaac needing service hours the night before, but she'd seemed hesitant.

Cheerful, feminine voices echoed from the back of the house. It was probably Lindsey and her aunt. Glancing past the ticking grandfather clock, he slid out the account book and put his envelope with the check inside, resisting the urge to thumb through the pages. A crash from the dining room made him jump.

Lindsey came around the corner, pushing a stroller with little boys hanging on. She came to a surprised stop.

"Hey."

"Hey," she returned. Her hair was up, her cheeks rosy, and her curious stare made Donovan's palms tingle. He realized he was holding the account book. His face warmed, and he fumbled inside the pages for his envelope. It fluttered to the floor with other papers. "I was just slipping next month's rent inside," he explained, trying to ignore the attraction that made him want to stare. "Your aunt prefers a check over a credit card."

Leo shouted, "Hey," and Archer darted over. Donovan picked up the loose papers, stuffed them inside the account book and set it on the counter. The phone rang. "I'll get it." Lindsey darted around him as Leo pushed the stroller across the room and crashed it into the clock. Donovan took control of the stroller and sat on the floor to explain to the twins how the back-wheels' locking mechanism worked, in a voice no louder than a whisper. Archer climbed into his lap, put a thumb in his mouth and listened intently.

Lindsey hung up the phone with a clatter.

"Thank you," she breathed, obviously exasperated. "I can take it from here."

Donovan looked up, secretly pleased Archer had taken a shine to him. The little boy's hair smelled like bubblegum, and he wondered if it was shampoo. "It's no problem," he assured her. "I'm happy to calm the chaos."

"Aunt Daphne really needs to use a cell phone number for the inn, but she's afraid it will be too overwhelming."

"You have an answering machine, right?"

"Yes." Lindsey glanced toward the register. "But it's outdated. She needs to use her cell phone or at least update the inn's website."

Archer and Leo chattered between themselves beside Donovan. He leaned back on his hands, eager to share his solution. "Daphne asked me about her website. She wants to create a social media presence for the place."

"Can you believe there aren't any social media accounts at all?" said Lindsey. "There isn't an online reservation system, either, just a landline."

Donovan reached to tousle Archer's hair. "It sounds like you need to hire a web designer or social media specialist. She could put her account books online, too."

Concern flitted across Lindsey's face.

"That would take extra money the inn doesn't have right now."

"That's too bad," said Donovan, trying to keep his face neutral.

Lindsey smoothed back her hair. "But we will when business picks up," she predicted in a determined voice. "Boys, are you ready to go on a walk?"

"Walk!" they cheered. Donovan got to his feet. "I'm on my way to the library to sit with my niece during Storytime. Would you like to come?"

"Your niece?" Lindsey seemed interested.

"Technically, she's my cousin's daughter, but he's like a brother, so…"

Lindsey's eyes widened. "Do you mean Claire's daughter? I met your cousin's wife a week ago, remember?"

"Oh that's right," remembered Donovan. "With my mom and her posse."

"Posse?"

"Mom and Ms. Diane stick together and rope in anyone around them."

"Rope them into what?" Lindsey seemed amused. She reversed the stroller, and Donovan stepped to the front door to open it for her.

"Get-togethers, walks, volunteering, their

book club and whatever else they can do to entertain themselves when they're not monitoring me."

"They seem nice."

"Oh, they are," he relented. "Maybe I'm a little envious I don't have a posse to run around with, but they mean well."

Lindsey smiled. "I like Claire. She said her daughter is four?"

"Yes."

Lindsey leaned down to buckle in the twins who'd climbed into the stroller by themselves. "I promised Diane I would come by and see her shop, but maybe we should also go look at books."

"Books! Books!" shouted Leo. Donovan helped her maneuver the stroller down the stairs. "I think they need a playmate," Lindsey confessed as they started down the sidewalk. "Claire seems like a great mom."

"She is." Donovan decided to tell her the story. "Bradley was married to Emily's mother for a brief time. She died when she was a baby, and Claire was her best friend. She was raising Emily when she met Bradley, but he didn't know he had a daughter."

"I see." Lindsey's forehead rippled.

"It's not as complicated as it sounds. I'm

sure she'll explain it to you better than I have," Donovan promised.

"I think it's pretty great," Lindsey allowed. "Fathers are important."

"That's true."

"Are you close to your dad?"

"I suppose so." Donovan swung his hands as he recalled his childhood. "We always got along, and we hang out on weekends—with Bradley, most of the time—but yeah. My dad's a good man."

Lindsey smiled. "I'm happy to hear that. So's mine. He still calls every Sunday night to see how my week went." Donovan watched her glance at the twins and wondered what was going through her mind. Her boys didn't seem to have a relationship with their father. "So," she said, breaking the pause as the warm sun shined down, "what's this exciting hour at the library all about?"

"It's thirty minutes of story time, then arts and crafts. Emily loves it," Donovan explained.

"And she doesn't lose interest?"

"No, she's active, but she likes to read, and she's always looking for playmates. I bet she'll adore the boys."

"Maybe she can help keep them out of trouble." Lindsey hoped.

Donovan grinned as the boys waved at every car that rolled by. When they crossed the street to Southern Fried Kudzu, Lindsey ducked her head inside to sneak a peek at the menu and came back out smiling. Fortunately, Donovan was able to distract the twins from noticing any delicious scents wafting out the entrance so they didn't ask for snacks. He took everyone next door to Alabaster's, where Lindsey gazed through the windows at the handmade jewelry. "These are beautiful." Before he could agree, Diane came outside. She gave Lindsey a friendly hug. "I saw you through the front window. I'm so glad you're here. Why don't you come in?"

"Oh no, I couldn't right now." Lindsey flushed.

"I can watch the boys for a minute," Donovan insisted. "Go right ahead."

Shooting Donovan a thankful smile, Lindsey followed her new friend into the store. She stopped in delight when the fragrances of candles drifted over her senses. "This is beautiful," she breathed, examining the room with wide eyes.

"I have cooking and baking gifts in the back," Diane said. "Do you like flavor-infused olive oils?"

"I do," admitted Lindsey.

"Claire makes my oil cruets." Diane pointed around the rest of the room. "Candles in that corner, cards and local books in the middle and jewelry up front." Lindsey stepped up to an earring display. "Those are from a local artist who makes her own paper and rolls it into jewelry," Diane explained.

"They're cute." Lindsey picked up a pair of earrings in red and green. She glanced outside. "Can you put these on hold for me? I'll come back."

"I sure will, honey." Diane took them from her and carried them to the register.

"Thank you."

"Thank *you*," Diane emphasized. "What else can I do? How is business at the inn?"

"The book club meetings will help. Thank you for that."

"I don't mind moving it from my shop. The inn is more comfortable, and your treats are better."

Lindsey chuckled. "I better go save Donovan," she said, remembering the boys. Diane looped her arm through hers to walk her out.

"While we're thanking each other, I'm glad you're here to help your aunt. She's a little blue sometimes. Since Jim left us."

"I know. We all miss him."

Diane stopped before opening the door. She eyed Donovan and the twins. "And I'm glad to see Donovan out and about instead of holed up in his office. I think Vi is grateful you've moved to town, too, and not just because Daphne needed help."

Lindsey flushed at the obvious hint. There was no point in denying the man waiting outside was appealing, but it was too complicated to explain why a romance between them wouldn't happen.

After they waved goodbye to Diane, Donovan led Lindsey the rest of the way down the street, pointing out his favorite landmarks. A block later, he pulled the stroller to a halt at a sign in front of a freshly painted white clapboard building with a pitched roof. A plaque designated it the founder's museum. "This looks like an interesting place," remarked Lindsey.

"It actually used to be our library. My cousin restored it back to the old schoolhouse it once was."

"He did a great job." Lindsey studied a flyer showing children at play and looked beyond the corner of the museum. "Is there a playground back there?"

"Almost," Donovan replied. "They're building one, and I bet the boys will enjoy it."

"That will be a lot of fun," Lindsey acknowledged. "What's in the museum?"

"Photographs, journals and work from local artists. We moved the library to a brick building that used to be a storage warehouse for peanuts and cotton in the old days. It's just as historic but has more room. The Chamber of Commerce meets there now, too."

"I'm surprised the book club doesn't."

"Mom and Diane like to keep it intimate. The new library's too big. They used to do it out at our house, but we live out of town, and it's too far for some members, like Ms. Olivia."

"I'm excited they're moving it to the Azalea Inn. We agreed to do a brunch for them every month, and they'll pay for it with membership dues." Lindsey beamed in the sunshine.

"I hope it helps out." Donovan saw her cast a look of curiosity his way. "I know the inn's been struggling the past couple years," he admitted.

"It's true," Lindsey allowed. "Your staying in the cottage helps."

"I enjoy it, and I love being closer to work."

"You don't mind the boys?" Lindsey wondered.

"No, of course not." Donovan said nothing about the trophy or that he tried to make sure the cottage door was locked now.

"I still intend to find a way to make up for what happened to your friend's trophy."

Looking away, his head was full of thoughts about Ryan's charity. After a few steps pushing the stroller, Lindsey misread his silence and asked, "So what happened to your friend? I can tell you cared about him a great deal."

Donovan tensed up, so he waited a few moments before speaking. "Ryan had addictions. Unfortunately, they got the best of him."

"I'm sorry. It can be so hard to help other people with serious things. Even family."

Donovan nodded in agreement. He hadn't been able to help Ryan. His heart sank, so he shifted his mind to Judge Sheldon and his son. Maybe if she liked his idea, she could help him convince Daphne. "You need someone to help with the inn's website and social media, right?"

Lindsey glanced at him sideways. "Right, but the inn's on a budget, remember? I'm not even getting paid a living wage yet."

"I have a friend," he began earnestly, "whose grandson needs to put in service hours."

"Like for Boy Scouts?"

"No, not like that," chuckled Donovan. He squinted at the library ahead looming with adventures and daydreams inside. "His grandson made a mistake and was involved in a car accident. He's been ordered to do community service, and I happen to know he's very good with computers."

Lindsey met Donovan's gaze with interest. "Do you think he could help us out?"

"I think so." Eagerness swelled in Donovan's chest. "He could update the inn's website for free and teach Daphne how to use some of the more popular social media apps for her audience."

"That'd be great." Lindsey gave her head a slight shake as if in disbelief. "It's so nice of you."

He smiled, pleased, but resisted the urge to reach out for her hand and give it a squeeze.

"I'm glad you think it's a good idea. I've spoken to Daphne about it, but she was unsure."

"I'll talk to her," Lindsey promised. "You're a good guy, Donovan."

"I like to think so." He hoped she wouldn't ask any more about Ryan. A part of him didn't want her to know how badly he'd failed a friend. Donovan was surprised when they reached the library doors. The walk had gone fast, and he was disappointed. He wanted to spend more time with her. More time than in the dining room of the Azalea Inn during breakfast. More time than tossing the ball to the boys in the backyard. But that wasn't a smart idea. She had children, not to mention a new career, and family back in Texas, plus he had designs on the inn she was so fond of. *Some good guy*, he thought wistfully to himself.

Lindsey parked the stroller beside the front doors and ducked under Donovan's arm while he held the door open. His heart hurtled over his rib cage when she shot him an appreciative smile. He inhaled the comforting fragrance of homemade bread and something melon-like that was so different than her boys'. There was no bubblegum in this woman's heart, nothing sticky or artificial about her at all.

* * *

Lindsey stepped into the library delighted to see Claire Ainsworth in the lobby with a blond-haired, brown-eyed little girl dancing in circles around her legs. "Lindsey!" Claire called out in delight. Completely ignoring Donovan, she gave Lindsey a light embrace. "I should have called you about today. I'm sorry I didn't think of it." She grinned at Donovan. "You're smarter than you look."

"Donovan mentioned it when I was on my way out the door with the boys," Lindsey explained. "I think they'll love Storytime."

"Uncle Don!" cried the little girl at their feet. She looked from Donovan to the twins. Leo and Archer stood oddly silent between Donovan and Lindsey. She tried to nudge them forward, but Archer backed into Donovan's leg and stuck his thumb in his mouth. Claire looked at Lindsey with an amused grin and dropped to her knees. "Hi, boys. This is Emily. She came to listen to a story today. Did you?"

"I have books," Leo informed her.

She dropped her jaw as if impressed. "You do?"

Lindsey leaned over and smiled at Emily.

"Hello, Emily. I'm Miss Lindsey. This is Leo and Archer. Can you say hi, Archer?"

Archer grinned around his thumb. Leo said, "Hi."

Emily pointed to her shirt. "I have a unicorn. Uncle Don, where's my horse?"

"You left it in my car," he told her, smiling.

Claire eased herself up from the floor. "I appreciate you sitting with her today," she told Donovan. "She requested your company, and since I have an order to fire in the kiln, I didn't think you'd mind as long as you didn't have to be in court."

"I don't," Donovan assured her. "Mrs. Lewis is minding the office."

Claire turned to Lindsey. "It's really nice seeing you again, but I better get back to work. Maybe we can go to lunch sometime."

Lindsey smiled in surprise. She hadn't had any time to make friends since she'd arrived in Kudzu Creek. "I think we could work something out."

"Oh, also," added Claire, "if you ever need someone to watch the boys, I would be available a few hours a day, if you'd be interested in exchanging babysitting time."

Lindsey brightened. "Help with the boys would be a blessing, and I wouldn't mind watching Emily sometimes," she assured Claire. "I have a few hours in the middle of most days."

"That'd be great for me." Claire watched the children chatter with each other. "Maybe we can give it a try next week." Donovan shuffled his feet. A few more children skipped by with their parents. "I'll let you get to Storytime," said Claire.

"Books!" shouted Leo, and Lindsey shushed him. After waving goodbye to Claire, she took the boys by their hands as Donovan led Emily to the children's section. The old warehouse was partitioned off by shelves in different sizes. In a far corner beneath big industrial lights, a thick carpet was laid out. Pillows and picture books made it inviting. A librarian was already seated on the rug, chatting with the children. As soon as Leo spotted her, he ran forward with Emily at his heels. Lindsey led Archer to a spot near the edge of the carpet and stepped back to give him room. He looked at her anxiously, and she gave him a small wave. Donovan took one of the hard chairs lining the carpet's edge. He leaned forward with his arms on his knees. Deciding to let Archer acclimate at his own speed, Lindsey slipped down beside him to watch.

"I think Archer's a little anxious," Donovan observed in a whisper when she was seated. It was nice of him to care. He was warm, smelled good and already felt like a trusted friend.

Archer looked over, and Donovan gave him a thumbs-up. "You're a big boy," he called in a loud whisper. The child shifted his glance to Lindsey. "You're fine," she assured him. Emily and Leo took seats in the front row and whispered between themselves, although it was primarily Emily doing the talking and Leo listening. *Perhaps he's met his match,* Lindsey thought. She peeked at Donovan long enough to admire him again. He was attractive, fit and dressed well, but he didn't mind getting dirty or dropping to the floor to play with the kids. There was something charming and reassuring about that. Not to mention Vi Ainsworth was a darling, which reminded Lindsey of her mother's admonition to watch how a man treated his mother. Donovan seemed to love his mom as much as Lindsey loved her own. In fact, he seemed to worship Vi although he'd looked sheepish when she popped into the Azalea Inn to check on him with all of her gang. Lindsey chuckled to herself, remembering his little blush.

"What?" he whispered as the librarian captured the children's attention with a theatrical voice and the first page of a book.

"You seem to fit in wherever you go," Lindsey observed in a quiet voice.

"I fit into the library?"

She nudged him with her elbow, surprised to find herself flirting with him. "You fit right into Kudzu Creek, the inn and even the library. Daphne told me you volunteer at the church's food pantry on the weekends once a month."

"There're people in this county that need a little help." Donovan seemed confused that service to the community was something to be admired.

"You like to help others." Lindsey studied him. "Simple, everyday people. It's commendable, considering you could live in a big city and work in a skyscraper."

He offered her a meek smile. "I guess that's why I became a lawyer. Not everyone knows how to advocate for themselves in emergency situations."

"Well, thank you for helping me with the boys in my emergencies."

"No problem." He winked at her. "It's easy to like them."

Lindsey wondered if he liked her, too, then realized that was beside the point. He was an ambitious bachelor content to manage his successful business and dote on his mother. The last thing he'd be interested in was a single woman living under her aunt's roof baking biscuits to support herself—even if he did like kids. She sat back, but she couldn't relax completely with him beside her. His leg grazed hers every few minutes, and his cedar aftershave wafted through the air every time he moved. It made her feel dizzy. Her arms, she realized, felt empty, even with two boys to care for. Or maybe it was her heart.

Lindsey exhaled, reminding herself to pay attention to the twins. One little distraction was all it took for Leo and Archer to wreak havoc in a harmless situation. Individually, they could get themselves into some major pickles, but together, they were double trouble. She glanced at the bookshelves around the children's area and hoped they were bolted to the floor.

She looked at the man beside her again. What was she doing on a playdate with Donovan? She had to help Aunt Daphne turn the business around. She had to raise her boys. There were necessary steps she needed to take to make her dreams come true. She couldn't be distracted by another man who seemed to have it all together and who wouldn't have time for her. Donovan Ainsworth did have it all together, and that meant he was probably the kind of man who didn't make allowances for relationships. Lindsey moved over a few inches so their legs didn't touch.

She liked it too much. Which was dangerous to her heart.

Chapter Five

On Thursday, Donovan walked into Southern Fried Kudzu and the scent of coffee and
burgers flooded his head. When he scanned
the crowd, he spotted Judge Sheldon and
Bradley jawing about something in the back
of the room. Donovan maneuvered to the register, where McKenzie Price was waiting with
a friendly smile on her face. The local wait-
ress who went by "Mac" had been a few years
behind him in high school, but they'd become
friends since she'd worked in the café.

"Is the lunch rush over?"

"Almost." Mac glanced over her shoulder,
and Donovan watched Barney flip something
on the grill. "What'll you have?"

Without looking at the menu, Donovan

said, "I'll take beans and rice with greens and a tall glass of tea."

"Sweet?" she clarified, although she already knew the answer.

"Always." He smiled.

Mac motioned toward the tables with her chin. There was a smudge of yellow on her cheek that looked like mustard. "Your friends have been waiting on you for a half hour. I'll bring it out."

"Thanks, Mac." Donovan hurried over to the table. Bradley pushed out a chair for him with his toe.

"Running late?" asked his cousin.

"New case."

"About what?"

Donovan gave him a close-lipped smile.

"Hope no one's hurt," Bradley offered.

Judge Sheldon growled, "I hope they weren't texting."

"Speaking of that," said Donovan, remembering his first order of business, "I spoke to Lindsey and Daphne about your grandson. They need help building a website for the inn. They also need an online reservation system, so I was able to convince them to give him a shot."

Judge Sheldon beamed. "Wonderful! That

would be great for him to see how a business is run."

"I think so, too," Donovan agreed. "There's a small office off to the side of the reservation desk in the lobby. Isaac can work in there."

Bradley rubbed his chin. "Isaac Sheldon. He's your grandson?"

Judge Sheldon bobbed his head in affirmation. "Yes, he graduated from high school last year but decided not to go to State when he didn't make the jazz band."

"That's unfortunate," Bradley observed. "Does he have any other plans?"

"Not yet." The judge frowned.

A picture of Ryan flashed in Donovan's mind. "Tell him if he has any problems he can come to the cottage and talk to me." The judge seemed humbled by Donovan's offer. But was it enough? "And my office is just down the street."

Judge Sheldon's face took on a rosy hue. "I appreciate your efforts, Ainsworth. I'll have him call Daphne this evening. How is the Azalea?"

Donovan loosened his tie and sat back in his chair. "They've been busy this week. I mean, last week was slow, but it picked up." He'd been paying close attention. It was hard not to with Lindsey skipping into his thoughts every free moment. His chest had started doing odd spirals every time he bumped into her.

"And the weekend's almost here," mused Bradley, snapping Donovan back to attention. Mac brought out Bradley's meatball sub, and then she passed Donovan his beans and rice.

"Weekends are busy for inns," the judge said. "Not that I've seen the Azalea Inn with much traffic since Jim died."

"It seems to be picking up since Lindsey moved in and became the chef," Donovan observed.

Bradley wiped his chin with a napkin while holding his loaded sub in the air. "They're not the only old business that might disappear. They've finally decided to demolish the old Blankenship barn."

Donovan looked at his cousin with interest. "That old farmhouse down highway ninety-one?"

Judge Sheldon grunted. "The grandkids have been fighting over that property for years. Finally been ordered to sell the house with the land."

"It's been boarded up forever," reflected Donovan.

Bradley nodded. "It's falling apart, that's for sure. I hear they're going to bulldoze the barn, sell the house and split the proceeds."

"It's a shame." Donovan frowned. "I kind of like seeing it whenever I drive by. It reminds me of an old grandpa looking out for me on my way home."

Bradley sighed. "Another one bites the dust, but at least downtown has been revitalized."

Donovan took a bite of his food. Bradley had done a good job updating the old Azalea. He swallowed. "You don't think turning the inn into a halfway house would be bad for the community, do you?"

"No, I think it'd show we care. Most of the properties on that street are being sold to businesses anyway. Even Parker and Associates is considering buying one and using it as an office."

"That's interesting," Donovan mused.

The judge grunted again. "I hate to see all of the old homes reoutfitted."

Donovan understood, but Pebble Stretch Road was already on its way to becoming another main thoroughfare through Kudzu Creek. Bradley crumpled a napkin. "Claire thinks the Blankenship property would be a great site for a co-op farm."

"A farm?" Donovan repeated.

"Yes. She doesn't like to drive so far down to the u-pick places for her strawberries and tomatoes every year. Not all of us have the time."

"I happen to enjoy doing that on the weekends." Judge Sheldon smacked his lips.

"It's not a bad idea," admitted Donovan. "I bet Lindsey would appreciate having something like that nearby."

Bradley gave him a funny look. "Claire likes her a lot. Apparently, they're going to start swapping childcare."

"Once a week or so, I heard. I was there."

"At the library?" Bradley asked.

"Yes, when she dropped off Emily the other day," Donovan replied.

"Oh, Emily told me all about it. Archer and Leo made quite an impression."

"I'm glad they had a chance to meet," said Donovan. "We took them to the inn afterward, and Lindsey gave them snacks before I took Emily home."

Lindsey had been amazing. She'd already prepped dinner service, so she was able to focus all of her attention on the children during the hour they played together. She offered them apple slices to dip in peanut butter, played soccer on the back lawn, then lined up pebbles in a long line on the driveway with them and pretended it was a highway for acorns.

"I can't imagine working with children underfoot," Judge Sheldon pointed out.

"She keeps them out of the way the best she can," Donovan assured him, "but it doesn't work out all of the time." He told them about the boys' nefarious deeds in the cottage. Just then, Mac showed up to refill their drinks.

She gave Donovan a curious stare. "I heard you were living at the Azalea now."

"We were just talking about it," he admitted.

"My friend is coming into town and looking for a place to stay while she visits."

"I definitely recommend it," Donovan blurted out before he realized what he was doing.

After Mac walked away, the judge gave him a quizzical look. "You can't buy the Azalea Inn if you're helping them get business, you know."

Donovan shrugged. "With two boys wreaking havoc, I'm not sure how much return business they'll get, but they're harmless. It doesn't bother me."

"It could be a problem for the Winthrop wedding."

"Winthrop?" Donovan raised a brow.

Judge Sheldon nodded. "Winthrop told my wife they were thinking about having their son's wedding there. The last venue fell through, and the bride's beside herself."

"Hmm," murmured Donovan pretending he wasn't concerned. A wedding would bring in a lot of cash.

"It'd be a nice place for an event." Bradley glanced at Donovan. "We don't have a lot of wedding venues here in Kudzu Creek."

"I supposed it'd be good for business," allowed the judge, but he glanced at Donovan with caution.

Donovan's heart dipped. If the Azalea Inn's business took off, that meant he'd have to rethink it becoming the halfway house. He'd set a goal to start the charity as soon as his business in town was up and running. Sensing his reluctance, Bradley asked, "Have you spoken to Daphne about your plans to buy the inn if she declares bankruptcy?"

"Not exactly."

"I'd like to come have a look at it myself," admitted Judge Sheldon with interest.

Donovan appreciated his mentor's support.

"That's not a bad idea. I'd like to show you some of my plans."

"But of course, if they start having weddings there…" Bradley sat back. "Weddings generate a lot of income. If they can make enough with those and their kitchen, they may be able to catch up with the bank payments in time."

Shrugging, Judge Sheldon said, "Perhaps." Ever the optimist, Bradley seemed to disagree. Donovan felt torn. He wanted his friends at the inn to be successful, but that meant his plans would be put on hold again. His emotions twisted, and he tried to sort them out.

Judge Sheldon dropped the remnants of a hamburger and wiped his hands on his napkin. "I asked Daphne about her niece last week, and she told me she was divorced. Said she hadn't been married more than a few months."

"He was an astronomer," Donovan supplied, "and they were married a couple years I believe."

"Does their father ever see them?"

Lindsey hadn't said much about her ex, and the twins didn't seem to have a scheduled time where they saw him. "I don't know."

Donovan noticed that Bradley looked troubled. His cousin had not known he had a daughter until she was almost three years old. "I'm sure she's worked out something fair," said Donovan. "She's generous." She was fair. And beautiful. In fact, he found her quite remarkable.

Something in his heart clicked like a light switch and made it glow. Focus. He had the charity to worry about. Restitution to make. "Regardless she seems to be doing just fine on her own."

Bradley shot him a look like he'd just committed a little perjury.

Aunt Daphne came into the kitchen before sunrise, just as Lindsey was pulling breakfast ingredients out of the refrigerator. Her aunt's purple bandanna held back her silvery-gray curls, and her cheeks were flushed with her usual enthusiasm. She tucked her hands inside the bib of her overalls. "Good morning, sunshine!"

Lindsey dropped a chunk of Gruyère cheese onto the butcher block counter. "You've been into the coffee bar," she guessed.

"Better," replied her aunt. "I just checked my emails." Aunt Daphne hopped up onto the tall stool that Archer perched on to eat his snacks. "Guess who's hosting a wedding?"

Lindsey stared in surprise. "The Azalea? Here?"

Her aunt grinned. "That's right. The Winthrop boy has decided to get married at the Azalea Inn in two months."

"That's wonderful news!"

"The azaleas will still have some color, and the roses will be in full bloom."

"They already have buds," gushed Lindsey.

"We can board up the firepit," decided Aunt Daphne. "And I'll get Bradley Ainsworth to freshen up the trellis."

Lindsey imagined the backyard full of flowers and strings of twinkle lights. "We can set up rows of white chairs, but we'll have to rent them," she said, stopping as daunting requirements rained down on her head.

"Don't worry about that right now." Aunt Daphne dismissed her concerns. "We'll pass that cost on to the bride as part of the late fee."

"Eventually, you could buy some of your own."

"Yes," agreed Aunt Daphne, "if things work out." She exhaled. "This may very well turn the tide for us, Lindsey."

Lindsey edged around the counter and gave her aunt a hug. "I told you everything would be okay. No matter how dark things look, there is always a way out. Just look how you answered my prayers when I had no idea where to go."

"I don't look at it that way," laughed Daphne. "I know you think I'm helping you out, but I needed you even more."

Lindsey grabbed her favorite skillet and scurried over to the stove. "How many guests do you expect this weekend?"

"Counting Donovan? Nine."

"That's great," cheered Lindsey, "and you have book club next week."

"Yes." Daphne reached for the cheese, while Lindsey unwrapped fresh sausages from the Peachtree Market. "Did I tell you about Judge Sheldon's grandson?"

Lindsey nodded. "Did you speak to him?"

"He called last night."

"He'll be great with the website," gushed Lindsey. "Donovan says he's a whiz."

"Yes, and I'm so excited I may not charge Donovan for meals anymore. This young man sounds like he knows what he's doing. He promised he can update our website and start accounts on Facestory and TippiTok."

Lindsey chuckled at her aunt's mispronunciation of the social media sites. "That should help spread the word."

"I hope so. It's nice of Donovan to recommend the boy, even though I know it's for community service."

"He can't be that bad a guy if Donovan suggested him," Lindsey insisted. She couldn't help but think of Donovan's loyalty to his friends—especially his friend who'd passed away. She reached for the toaster. "Can I ask you something? Do you know anything about his friend who died in high school? "

Her aunt scrunched her forehead. "I'm not sure."

"Donovan has a trophy," explained Lindsey. "He said it was a friend's from high school. A boy named Ryan."

Aunt Daphne's mouth turned down. "Oh, Ryan Boyington. Yes, I remember that boy. He was Donovan's friend?"

"Best friend in school for a while."

"Ryan Boyington was a rabble-rouser," Aunt Daphne said in a low tone.

Lindsey looked at her in disbelief. "It's not like you to speak ill of someone."

"He was nothing but trouble." Aunt Daphne shook her head with honest regret. "I don't know what he got up to in high school, but he was the prime suspect around here for several years every time a home or car was broken into."

"That doesn't sound like someone Donovan would be friends with."

"It doesn't make sense to me, either," confessed Aunt Daphne. "They couldn't have been that close, or Donovan would have ended up on the other side of the law." Scooting off the stool, she added, "I think Ryan passed away ten or twelve years ago."

"How sad."

"Yes," agreed Aunt Daphne. "I know it devastated the family because they were good folks, but most people said it was good riddance." Daphne clucked her tongue. "They weren't too kind about it, but you reap what you sow, I guess." Water echoed from the pipes upstairs, and she looked up. "It sounds like the Tabor couple is up and at 'em. I'll go check the coffee bar—again," she teased.

"You do that," laughed Lindsey. She started warming English muffins after her aunt disappeared. The house hummed while dawn glowed through the windows. *Reap what you sow?* Lindsey's heart snagged. She'd given up every hope and dream along with all of her love to someone she trusted, and what'd she have to show for it? No partner and no sweetheart, unlike the Tabors and the other happy couples who came to enjoy the Azalea Inn together. Donovan's grin crept into her thoughts, and she pushed it right back out. No, she was alone, reaping what she'd sown, a martyr to her own cause. She sighed and reached for the butter dish. But she never made the same mistake twice. The twins were a blessing and a bonus she'd never regret, but her dreams had to come first now and she'd never trust anyone with them again. Love would have to wait. It couldn't sidetrack her. But it might help if she'd quit looking forward to seeing her favorite guest every morning.

Everyone emptied out of the dining room after breakfast except Mr. Tabor, who was insatiably curious about where Donovan was heading and why he lived at the inn. The man cornered him in the lobby to share a graphic story about a twenty-five-car pileup he'd seen on a freeway in a Wyoming blizzard. Donovan listened while trying to keep a patient look of interest on his face.

He saw Lindsey watching them with amusement as she cleared buffet dishes off the sideboard. When she returned from the kitchen, Mr. Tabor had disappeared, and Donovan was refilling a cup at the coffee bar for the office. He looked over his shoulder when she whipped off the first tablecloth. "You're free," she observed.

"Do I really look like a lawyer?" he asked.

"Maybe like one of those billboards promising million-dollar settlements," she teased.

He cringed. "We're not all bad." He popped a lid onto his cup and stuffed two packets of sugar into his pocket.

"Well, I haven't seen you chasing any ambulances yet," she joked.

He laughed. "I'll leave that to Kessler."

"Who's that?" she wondered out loud.

"Someone I've been meaning to bring over and introduce to the boys." Donovan glanced up the stairs deciding to keep his favorite dog a mystery for now. "Where are they?"

"Still asleep. I checked the monitor." She looked overhead as if the twins were listening. "Every ten minutes."

Donovan chuckled. "Don't worry, the cottage is locked, and I made sure the broom on the porch is put away so they can't whisk the firepit."

"They'll find something to stir it with,"

she predicted, "just like they found Aunt Daphne's lipstick yesterday and graffitied the wall." She gave Donovan a sudden, long look. Before he could respond, she slid between the tables in his direction, making his stomach do handsprings. She surprised him by spinning him around. "You're rumpled." She smoothed down the back of his collar.

"Thank you," he stammered. "I have some pretrial motions to present today."

"Will you be back in time for dinner?" She released him, and he turned to meet her eyes. "I mean," she began, cheeks coloring, "I don't have you on the list. We're a little distracted with a travel blogger coming in this weekend."

Donovan raised the cup to his lips to hide the fact his heart was skipping at her words. "I wasn't planning on it, but if you're going to miss me…"

She gave a half laugh. "I just needed to know. Reservations are picking up, and I want to keep the pantry stocked."

"Right." His grin melted away at his senseless flirting. Something was happening here. Business picking up was good news for her, but not for him. He scanned the room, imagining it with an extralong dining table that could seat a dozen young men. They could eat together there. Talk. Inspire one another.

"I hope your motions go well today, then."

"Thanks, and I don't think I'll make it for dinner," Donovan informed her. "I have a late appointment, and I need to go over some things." He needed space from these feelings. They lit up like Christmas lights every time she walked into a room.

"For your case? You seem to have a lot on your mind."

"No, it's for my charity." Donovan felt a sudden lump in his throat.

"Right. What kind of charity is it again?"

"A home for young men."

"Oh," Lindsey said with interest. "And this will be your baby?"

"It's going to be," he explained, torn over whether or not to share the details. Her brows furrowed at his short answer. Something tweaked Donovan in the center of his chest. "Do you remember the trophy?" he said.

"Yes."

He released a breath. He was a lawyer and a Christian. Honesty always was the best policy. Her aunt's inn was failing, and he needed it. For Ryan. "I want to start a charity to remember Ryan. It'll be a halfway house for young men trying to get back on their feet after addiction. They'll go through a drug rehab program then move into the charity's halfway house that provides shelter with ongoing job and educational opportunities. It's still in the planning stages."

Lindsey's face went pale. "That's admirable," she breathed. "Here in Kudzu Creek?"

"That's right." He pushed the guilt away. A charity was…charitable. "I've been researching properties here in town for the best location," he said at last.

Lindsey looked around the dining room, and he could almost see the gears turning in her brain. "You're not considering the inn, are you?"

He held her gaze. "I thought I'd check out how business was going while I rented a room. You know, in case the property goes up for sale."

There was a slight pause as they stared at one another.

"The property isn't going up for sale," Lindsey replied without blinking.

Donovan shifted his weight and glanced up the stairs. "I know it isn't yet, but I'm looking around for a property, and since I needed a place to stay, I thought I'd see how things were going for your aunt."

Lindsey's hands went to her hips. "You won't have to worry about that, Donovan, because the inn is going to be fine."

"I'm glad things are going well at the moment," he insisted, but his tight throat made him sound hoarse, like he wasn't quite telling the truth.

"Are you?" She pressed her lips together. "May I ask what you were doing in Aunt Daphne's papers the other day?"

"What?"

"The account book. The register. You were looking through it before we went to the library."

Donovan felt like someone had thrown him on the witness stand. "I was putting the next month's rent inside," he said staunchly. "You can ask her yourself."

From the look in her eyes, Donovan knew that she would. The woman had trust issues a mile long and just as wide. "Like I said," Donovan repeated, "I hope things work out for you here. I'm just considering my options, is all."

"I'm sure Aunt Daphne will be comforted knowing if her business falls apart you'll be happy to take it off her hands." Lindsey strode off, leaving him speechless.

Donovan hadn't meant to upset her; in fact, that's why he'd waited so long to mention it. He dabbed his forehead with the back of his hand, knowing he should have explained himself better. It's what he did for a living after all. He dropped the to-go cup back onto the counter, cravings gone. Lindsey focused on nothing but her boys and her job. He'd met people like that before.

She was in survival mode.

He heard a thump up above and guessed it was one of the twins running up and down the hall between the guests' rooms. Leo must have escaped the attic suite. He headed for the door. He had a schedule to keep. Whether or not Lindsey trusted him was not his problem. It wasn't like they were in a relationship.

"Uncle Don!"

He turned as he stepped outside. Leo waved at him from between the balusters. He'd picked up Emily's name for Donovan after the library playdate. Donovan gave him a friendly wave before shutting the door behind him with a click. He wished he had time to play this morning, but his schedule was waiting.

ely needed worship and counsel. Though
eeing Donovan made it hard to concentrate.

He'd been distant but polite on Saturday,
playing with the twins in the backyard as if
nothing had happened the day before. As if
he hadn't informed her it was his intention to
take over the Azalea Inn.

Lindsey forced herself to rehearse the
menu, but it was hard to focus. She needed
to put out a nice breakfast for the weekend
guests, especially for the travel writer, but
she couldn't help but mull over Donovan, and
how—with a smile on his handsome face—he
didn't let anything get in his way. What had
he really been doing at the reservation counter going through Daphne's account book?
Lindsey's heart dropped. She knew all she
had to do was ask Aunt Daphne about it, but
that would lead to a conversation concerning
him, and Lindsey's feelings about him were
jumbled right now. She tightened her grip on
the stirring spoon. But she knew one thing
for certain. Donovan would have to find another home for his charity project.

"Mommy?" Leo's sleepy voice made Lindsey jump. She looked and saw he'd slunk
down the back staircase and was slumped
on the bottom stair.

Chapter Six

Lindsey tried not to slam dishes around as she fried country ham and stirred grits. Waking the boys this early wouldn't be a good idea. She'd had a lot to deal with since taking off after serving breakfast yesterday. For the first time, she'd driven the boys to Grace Point Chapel where her aunt and uncle had worshipped for years. Aunt Daphne had given Lindsey a concerned look during the service as she sat stiffly, attempting to listen to the sermon. The truth was, Lindsey was trying not to stare at the back of Donovan's head. He was sitting several rows ahead of them beside his mother and father. Aunt Daphne had taken the news of his interest in the inn going bankrupt with a grain of salt, but Lindsey desper-

"Good morning, baby," she said, trying not to panic at the interruption. He sprawled over the bottom step and clutched his blanket. His cheeks looked red and splotchy.

"Are you okay?" After turning down the heat on the ham, Lindsey went to her son and laid a hand on his forehead. It felt blazing hot. "Oh, Leo, you have a fever," she whispered. He stared at her listlessly. She covered him with his blanket and hurried to the refrigerator to get a glass of cold juice. He only took a sip before she smelled ham burning. Lindsey dashed to the stove and turned off the heat, but it was too late. The meat was overdone which meant it would be dry.

"Mom."

Lindsey gave the grits a good stir. The spoon scraped over a gummy layer on the bottom. "Oh no, they're sticking!" She pushed them off the heat, exasperated. China clacked in the dining room, and Lindsey realized someone was already at the coffee bar. They still had over a half-dozen guests from the weekend, and only two would be leaving. She glanced at the clock. It was early, and Aunt Daphne had not checked in on her.

Leo made a whimpering noise, his way of demanding attention when he didn't have the strength to be boisterous. "Just a minute, baby," Lindsey said. He began to cry. Worried, she threw muffins into a basket and raced out to set them on the buffet. To both her discomfort and relief, it was not a weekend guest at one of the tables, but Donovan, staring out the window at the sunrise. Her breath hitched in her lungs when their eyes made contact, but she said nothing, abandoning the muffins on the buffet without a tea towel. From the kitchen, Leo began to howl.

"Good—"

Lindsey shot back through the kitchen door, cutting off Donovan's greeting. She knew, despite how wonderful he was with the boys, that it was just an obligation. He was just trying to make himself feel better about his plans. Rushing back to her baby on the stairs, Lindsey heaved Leo over her shoulder, then returned to the stove. She put the burnt piece of ham on the bottom of a platter and covered it with better slices. Careful not to dig up the bottom of the pot, she slopped the grits into a serving bowl. Leo felt like a boiling-hot sack of potatoes. She rearranged him, picked up the ham platter with her free hand, and elbowed her way into the dining room.

A visiting couple from Mobile were downstairs now, speaking in low tones. Lindsey pasted a smile on her face and raised the platter slightly in the air to assure them breakfast was on its way. Leo reared back and looked around the room, bumping her arm. "Mommy," he whimpered, and the platter slipped from her fingers. Lindsey tripped and came down on her knees while trying to keep from dropping her son. The platter crashed upside down with a deafening sound and splintered in half. Ham juices splattered everywhere.

"Mom!" Leo bellowed and began to cry. Stunned, Lindsey felt her stinging knees and the stares of the guests. Before she could collapse in despair, solid arms wrapped around her middle and pulled her to her feet. She inhaled cedar and the minty fragrance of toothpaste. When she looked, Donovan's eyes were close enough to see small brown rings around the green edges. Trees. Warm and tender trees.

"I'm fine," she mumbled, aware of the heat she felt where he held her.

"Are you sure?" She nodded.

Leo wiggled and leaned toward Donovan. "Here. Let me." Donovan cradled his arms beneath Leo, and the boy fell into him.

"He's sick," Lindsey explained. She heard a small gasp from the table beside her. Her guests looked concerned. "I'm sure it's not contagious," she assured them, mentally praying she was right.

"It's fine," Donovan promised her. "Are you?"

"Yes. I just need to clean this up, and then I'll—" Silverware clattered on the table. Leo sobbed. The grits would be cold and scorched. Panic started to take hold of her.

"I'll take him upstairs. Take your time." Donovan hurried away before she could think of any other solution.

"Oh, no!" a surprised voice cried out.

At the entrance to the dining room, Aunt Daphne stood like a statue. "I'm so sorry," Lindsey gushed. "I'll have something else out in a moment." The guests smiled with pity, but she saw a flicker of impatience. Another visitor came around the corner and stopped beside Aunt Daphne. Lindsey's heart dropped when she saw it was the travel writer. He had his phone in hand and looked eager to take a few pictures.

"We're running a little late," Aunt Daphne explained, and she directed him to the coffee bar. "We'll be right out."

Lindsey stooped to pick up the broken platter and ham, but Aunt Daphne shooed her away. "I got this," she said in a tight tone. "Why don't you find some fruit and something else from the pantry?"

Lindsey choked back a whimper. Her knees hurt, her baby was sick, and she'd ruined an important breakfast. There would be no pretty magazine pictures of the inn's tasty dishes. She raced back to the kitchen, grabbed yogurt and granola, then filled another platter with slices of melons, blueberries and raspberries. Meanwhile, the grits were hardening like cement on the stovetop. Her head whirled, but she was thankful for Donovan. Again.

Donovan was relieved when the alarm on his phone chimed with a reminder that it was time to take a break. He could hardly concentrate anyway. Remembering his promise to walk Kessler, he eased out of his chair and tucked his phone into his pocket. With a smile, Mrs. Lewis, his ever-efficient secretary, handed him messages on his way out the door. There was a call from his client in the hospital, and a return call from the real estate agent selling the Blankenship property, who he'd contacted out of curiosity.

Blinking in the bright sunlight, Donovan strolled up Creek Street and swung to the right as he rolled up his sleeves. He ducked under the shade of Knight's Pharmacy's blue sign and continued to the next building that contained a food pantry on one side and Judge Sheldon's personal office on the other side. The judge's assistant stood outside, holding Kessler by the leash and looking impatient. Donovan crouched and petted the dog, who licked him with enthusiasm. Laughing, he took the leash and started back down the street toward the small, circular green space in the middle of town. Kessler liked to roll in the grass under the flagpole and permit passersby to scratch his belly. The old dog nearly killed himself lunging the entire way on his stubby legs. Donovan stood in a narrow beam of shade cast by the tall flagpole after greeting Mac on her break from the café. After waving her off, he nodded at Laurel Murphy as she walked past with an important envelope tucked under her arm. The Kudzu Creek historical preservation board's president looked grim, which meant someone was changing things in town without her approval. He chuckled to himself.

"You need to get yourself a dog of your own."

Donovan turned to find Bradley in dress pants, which meant he'd just left Parker and Associates' office up the street.

"Why's that? I'm just being a good neighbor."

Bradley grinned. "Or trying to stay on the judge's good side for the next time there's an opening for district attorney."

"Oh, it's not like that," Donovan maintained. "I like the exercise, and he's at the county seat most days, so I told him I could do it. Where're you heading? Thought you'd be at Kudzu's."

Bradley shaded his eyes in the sunshine. "Actually I'm on my way to the Azalea Inn."

Donovan straightened with immediate concern. "Is everything okay?"

"As far as I know," Bradley said. "Why?"

Donovan shuffled his feet so Kessler did not sit on his shoes. "There was a disaster in the dining room this morning, but I left after taking Leo upstairs."

"Is he okay?"

"He's running a fever. Archer slept through it, but Lindsey was juggling Leo on her shoulder in the dining room and fell and almost dropped him."

Bradley's eyes narrowed. "That doesn't sound good. Is she okay?"

"Yes, they both are, although I bet her knees are black-and-blue. It caused a scene for the guests, and I don't think Daphne was happy."

"Emily isn't feeling well this morning, either." Bradley frowned. "I was supposed to take a look at an old trellis in the backyard for Daphne today. She wants me to replace the rotting parts and get it repainted."

Kessler crawled to his feet and began snuffling through the grass, stretching the leash. Donovan gave it some leeway. "For the wedding?"

Bradley nodded. "She said the Winthrops have reserved the inn. It's a done deal."

"Isaac Sheldon is supposed to start work there this week." Donovan tensed.

"It was nice of you to set that up." Bradley was always generous with praise. "It may seem like a small thing, but it only takes a few things to change a life."

Donovan relaxed. "Helping him out makes me feel better." He twisted the leash in his hand, wondering how long the dog would last in the heat. "I think things are looking even better for the inn," he admitted. "A travel writer is here."

"And the wedding will mean a good chunk of change."

"I hope it will cheer Lindsey up," Donovan allowed. "She was pretty upset this morning."

"Having kids can be stressful," Bradley pointed out. "It isn't good news for you, though, is it? Have you looked at any other real estate for your charity?"

"I called about the Blankenship land," Donovan divulged.

"How much do you think they want for it?"

Donovan shrugged. "I don't know. With all the acreage it would be more than the inn."

"I don't think the house is inhabitable."

Donovan gave Bradley a look of hopeful encouragement. "You're a contractor. Maybe you can take a look."

"Are you serious about it, then?"

"It's a bit of a drive from town, and to be honest, it has too much land."

"It might be good to have land for a group of young men to work."

Donovan sighed. "I suppose. I'd just imagined a place in town where they could walk to jobs at the market or diner."

"I can see that, too." Bradley gazed down the street. "I think transportation into town would be an issue, but either way, you'll find your house, just be patient. You'll know it when you see it."

I already have, thought Donovan. A large farmhouse in the country was a big investment. He grunted. "I've already found the perfect place."

"You're doing the right thing looking at the inn," Bradley said.

"Right. It's for Ryan. His house. It deserves to be in town."

"Ryan's House has a nice ring to it."

Donovan looked at him with interest. *Ryan's House*. The town should remember Ryan, not as a less-than-perfect person, but as someone who didn't have the resources to overcome his mistakes. "I think you've nailed it," Donovan decided. "Ryan's House is the perfect name."

Kessler brushed up against Donovan's leg, looking tired and hot. He crouched and ran his hand down the dachshund's quivering back. "Now I just have to figure out what to do."

Bradley made a noise of agreement. "You

really have your heart set on the Azalea, don't you?"

"I have my heart set on a lot of things," Donovan admitted. It surprised him when he said the words out loud. His cousin looked at him curiously, and he tried to laugh it off, but his chest flooded with emotions that he couldn't name. "What I meant was—"

"I think I know what—or who—you meant," Bradley teased.

"I haven't changed my mind about that," Donovan said emphatically. "She knows about the charity. I mentioned I was interested in buying the inn after foreclosure to her."

"How did that go over?" Bradley asked.

"That I wanted to buy the place where she's working?" Donovan held out his palms. "Not well."

"I can imagine."

"We haven't had a chance to really talk about it, but I have a feeling she's angry with me," Donovan confided.

"Well, sure. Where would she and the twins go if things didn't work out with the inn?" Bradley asked.

Donovan squinted at the climbing sun. "I don't know."

He was embarrassed to realize he'd never

thought about it. He'd only focused on what he needed, he and his charity.

Guilt washed over him. He cared about Lindsey and the twins. He really did. And he didn't want them to have to leave, not when they'd just settled down in Kudzu Creek. The thought startled him, but it was true. They were a part of his life now, and that was something he didn't want to change.

Chapter Seven

On Wednesday, the temperature started climbing early so Lindsey decided to make a gallon of lemonade after breakfast. She'd already baked petit fours and sugar cookies for the book club, and included her special blueberry muffins for Ms. Olivia. Leo had recovered enough to wander around the house, and Archer had only run a low grade fever for a day, so she took both twins outside for some fresh air until lunchtime. Afterward, Aunt Daphne herded them to the lounge, and Lindsey checked the inn's phone messages at the register. She spied the new web designer in the small office and ducked her head in.

"Hi, there."

A young man, just out of his teens, leaned back in surprise. He was slim like a string bean, with dark hair and horn-rimmed glasses. "Oh, hi, Miss—"

"You can just call me Lindsey," she chuckled. The boy moved to stand, and she held out a hand to stop him. "Please, don't. I didn't mean to interrupt you."

"I'm Isaac Sheldon," he said.

"I know." Lindsey smiled. "I heard you came in Monday and met with Aunt Daphne. How was your first day?"

"I started yesterday at home," Isaac admitted. "But I'm going to come in a few days a week to help." He motioned toward the computer.

Lindsey nodded. "I guess you've seen how old the website is."

"Yes, but that won't take long to update. I'm working on code for an online reservation system right now."

"That's fantastic. Can I get you anything?" Lindsey offered.

He flushed. "Oh no, I'm not really—I mean, it's no big deal. I'm just helping out Ms. Daphne a little."

Lindsey winked. "You're helping more than you know. Tell me if the twins get in your hair."

"They're cool," he assured her.

"So what about this month's book?" asked Diane. "What did y'all think?"

As some of the women chimed in with their thoughts, Claire grabbed a few petit fours. "Mmm, these are delicious, Lindsey."

"They are," agreed Mac. "They'd sell like crazy at the café."

"Thanks." Lindsey smiled. "I'll have to check out your tarts."

The women chattered about the book and other various things. Then, before she could stop herself, Lindsey blurted out, "Did you know Donovan was planning to start a half-way house?"

"Half a house?" asked Ms. Olivia with a frown.

"A halfway house," repeated Diane in a loud voice.

Donovan's mother nodded. "Yes, he's supported charities like that for years." She scooted her chair closer to Lindsey. "Donovan lost a close friend when he was young," she confided. "He's riddled with guilt and won't stop blaming himself."

"He mentioned it." Lindsey looked down at the table.

"So he's decided to start a charity of his own here in Kudzu Creek," Vi continued.

"Yes," Lindsey acknowledged, "but did you know he wanted to buy the Azalea Inn?"

No one at the table looked surprised. "Is this place for sale?" asked Ms. Oliva.

"No, no yet." Lindsey looked anxiously over her shoulder for Aunt Daphne. "I mean, things haven't been going so great the past couple years."

"Since Jim died," Vi finished in a sorrowful tone. She rested a hand on Lindsey's. "I'm sorry about your uncle."

"Thank you."

Vi studied her. "Donovan mentioned he liked the Azalea Inn after he moved in, and he heard your aunt was struggling, so it seemed like something to consider." She lifted one shoulder. "We all knew."

"There was a letter from the bank." Lindsey looked around the table.

"He told me," said Vi, "but Daphne had already mentioned it." The other women at the table looked interested, and Lindsey supposed Vi had tastefully kept the news of the bank's warning to herself.

"I was just caught off guard," Lindsey explained, "since he was staying here."

"I'm having my guesthouse done," his mother reminded her. "That's the reason why

he rented the cottage here, but yes, he feels
a connection to this place, so if things don't
work out he's going to make an offer and help
Daphne find another home." Vi's soft hazel
eyes looked concerned. "He isn't hoping the
inn fails, Lindsey. None of us are."

"It can't fail. It was Aunt Daphne and Uncle
Jim's dream."

Diane reached for the lemonade. "If she has
to give it up, she won't have to worry about
someone taking advantage of her. Donovan
will make sure to do right by her."

"It's not his fault business is slow in Kudzu
Creek this year, and he feels he's giving
Daphne a fair chance by staying in the cot-
tage," reiterated Vi.

"You're right," Lindsey relented. "He even
pays for extra meals."

"That's because he likes your cooking."
Claire smiled. "It's all he talks about when
he comes over." Lindsey felt herself blush.
"And by the way, you should come by sometime," Claire suggested. "You can give my
cooking a chance, although I'm sure it's not
as delicious as yours. Then you and the twins
can pit yourselves against Emily and Bradley
and Donovan in hide-and-seek."

The thought of playing hide-and-seek in

Claire's elegant Victorian home, known as the historic Henny House, cheered up Lindsey. "That does sound fun, but I can't imagine Donovan hiding under a laundry basket."

Vi chuckled. "He loved that game when he was little, and Emily gives him a chance to pretend he hasn't forgotten how to play."

"And he plays with her all the time," Claire assured them all. "I trust him completely."

As if on cue, the door to the inn swung open, and Donovan walked inside. He stopped short when he saw the women gathered around the table, and Lindsey noticed he held a leash with a pert, graying dachshund on the other end.

"Donovan," scolded his mother, "you can't bring a dog in here."

His gaze flitted to Lindsey. "I forgot you were having book club today." He looked down at the dog. "I was just walking Kessler for Judge Sheldon and thought I'd bring him over to meet the boys."

"*This* is Kessler?" Lindsey asked in amusement.

He lifted the leash. "This is Kessler."

Was this his way of apologizing for keeping his intentions secret? Lindsey looked at the adorable animal. "The boys love dogs," she admitted. She glanced toward the back. "They're with Daphne in the lounge, unless she's taken them outside."

Donovan glanced at the table of women, then led the dog away. A moment later, cries of delight echoed through the house just as Vi steered them back to the book discussion. "Guess he found them," Claire giggled.

Lindsey wished she could see the twins' faces. They'd be giddy the rest of the day. "It sure sounds like it," she agreed. Donovan had a way with children, and she couldn't resist someone who liked dogs as much as she did. She sensed Claire watching her and pretended to concentrate on the others' conversation. No matter how much she tingled when she was around him, Claire had to stay focused. Donovan was a wonderful man, but the bulldog of a lawyer wanted her aunt's inn.

After returning Kessler to Judge Sheldon, Donovan hurried to Southern Fried Kudzu to grab an iced coffee. Since Bradley's office was just two doors down from the café, he met Donovan again long enough to extend an invitation to Sunday lunch, then confessed Lindsey and the twins would be there as well. The upcoming little party distracted Donovan all afternoon, despite the caffeine rush. He'd waited too long to admit his interest in buying the Azalea Inn to Lindsey, and it'd resurrected a wall he'd pulled down from around her. It bothered him more than he wanted to admit. For some reason, he needed her to believe him when he said he wanted what was best for the inn. She'd given him a forgiving smile when he'd brought Kessler to meet the boys, but his gut told him it wasn't going to be enough.

When he finally locked the office door after work, Donovan knew what he had to do. Hopefully, she would understand and believe he wasn't doing anything to hinder Daphne from trying to save her business. A few rumbles of thunder announced a piercing rain shower, and without an umbrella, Donovan jogged home with water spattering his head and clothes. He juggled a messenger bag as he sprinted up the driveway to the cottage. Rain pounded on the small awning over the front door as he patted himself down for his keys, then dug through his bag. Water trickled down his back. He squeezed his eyes shut in frustration. He'd locked the office door and then...

Donovan searched the bag again. Thunder

pealed, and a flood of water cascaded off the roof, soaking him. He tucked the bag under his arm and eyed the inn. Taking a breath, he darted into the downpour and hurdled the stairs to the back porch. He considered parking himself there until a brisk wind rushed past the eaves. He shivered and reached for the door to the lounge, but through the panes, he saw couples playing cards inside. He couldn't march into the lounge, flinging water everywhere, then soak a chair while he figured out what to do. Donovan considered the entrance to the kitchen. Perhaps Lindsey was upstairs with the boys and hadn't started dinner yet. He let himself in, but in one small whiff, he knew bread was baking, and it made his mouth water.

The kitchen felt cozy after the chill of the rain. Lindsey stood at the stove, whisking something in a pot, with a contemplative look on her face. Her hair pulled back, her profile was in full view, and he admired her as his stomach did a funny thing that had nothing to do with the tantalizing aromas floating around the kitchen. Despite her circumstances, she was kind, generous and strong. He wondered what it would be like to be more than just a friend who helped her with her boys sometimes. A warm feeling settled over him, but he realized he was being foolish. Lindsey had children. He had his career. And there was a literal house between them.

Lindsey noticed him gawking like a fool and jumped. "Donovan!"

His mouth twitched. "Daydreaming over boiling pots, huh?"

She grinned, and he wondered if bringing Kessler over earlier had softened her heart after all. "I was concentrating on the baby monitor," she admitted, casting a glance at the small speaker sitting next to the stove. "The boys are stirring."

"Nap time's almost over, I take it?"

"Yes, and they had quite a rambunctious afternoon stomping all over the house." She turned off the stove and pushed the pot back. Donovan pulled out a stool as he slid out of his wet blazer. "You're soaking wet," she observed.

"Yes, I'm sorry. Do you happen to have a towel?"

She grabbed one and came around the counter, eyeballing him from head to toe. "Did you forget your umbrella?"

"It wasn't raining this morning. I had to run for it."

"Oh, wow," she chuckled. "I hope the old track skills kicked in." She glanced back at the stove. "I could have come and picked you up, you know."

"It's okay. It wasn't that bad until I reached the cottage and couldn't find my keys."

"You're locked out?"

"I am," he admitted sheepishly.

A teasing grin emerged on Lindsey's face. "The boys learned to lock the bedroom door upstairs," she shared in a grim tone. "That's been an interesting development."

Donovan laughed. "I bet." He swiped his dripping hair back from his face and realized his normally tight curls were loose and heavy ringlets. He cringed.

Lindsey handed him the towel with a peculiar expression. He must have looked awful with his curly hair dripping. His dress shirt clung to his shoulders. Pools of water collected at his feet. The kitchen fell silent except for the steaming appliances. When she raised her appraising gaze from the wet floor, he saw something in her eyes he couldn't name. "Sorry I'm making a mess in your kitchen," he stammered.

"Oh, don't worry about it. I'll just run a mop over the floor and it'll be fine."

Suddenly, Donovan couldn't stop himself. He slid off the stool and stood up.

"Lindsey, I want to offer you back the cottage." She stared at him in surprise. "I know your aunt gave it to me, but you were expecting it, and I realize you have more need of it than I do."

"You want to swap?"

"Yes," he offered. "I'm up before most guests, stay out most of the day, and Daphne has quiet hours posted at ten o'clock so I wouldn't have any problems getting the sleep I need. The cottage would give you more privacy with the boys," he added, "and you wouldn't have to stress so much about them bothering the guests."

"That's so kind of you." Lindsey swept her gaze around the well-stocked kitchen. "I don't know if—"

"You have your baby monitors," Donovan pointed out. "Daphne has the sofa in her office if you need to have them nearby while they're napping."

"They stay quiet and play on the floor in here sometimes...most of the time, if they're not upstairs," she said thoughtfully. "But they make so much noise running around the attic."

"Daphne keeps an eye on them when you're serving meals, right? So…"

Gratitude and what he hoped was trust seemed to flood Lindsey's eyes. "That's really nice of you to offer."

"Then, take me up on it," Donovan insisted.

Suddenly, the light in her eyes dimmed. "But Aunt Daphne relies on your rent," she said coolly.

"The attic suite is—"

"She makes a little more from the cottage," Lindsey finished.

"Oh." Donovan didn't want to live at the Azalea Inn with a beautiful chef who didn't think he was a man of his word. If he said he cared about people first, he needed to show it. "I'll just keep paying the same rate I'm paying now."

Her brows raised. "She won't ask you to do that."

"Why not?" Donovan shrugged. "It has just as much square footage—or more. I'd have the entire floor to myself. I'm closer to the dining room." His mind eagerly searched for more excuses. "There's better Wi-Fi for my computer," he added.

She frowned. "Does it not work well back there?"

"It's terrible," he teased.

"How about this? You talk to Daphne about it, and if she agrees, I'm fine with it."

"Thanks," he said. But she studied him as if he had an ulterior motive. He knew he had to clear the air between them. "I'm sorry I didn't tell you about Ryan's charity sooner." Lindsey looked away. It made something inside of him deflate. "I only checked in to see if I would want to make an offer to the bank."

"And do you?"

Donovan's cheeks warmed. "The answer is yes. I like it here." A water droplet rolled down the side of his forehead and fell onto the bridge of his nose. He ran his fingers through his hair to comb through the sopping-wet mess. "Even if I wasn't a guest, I could see myself living here." Still, Lindsey didn't seem satisfied. "I think it's a great property, and it'd be a perfect spot for Ryan's House—that's what I'm going to call it. Ryan's House."

"That's nice."

Lindsey sounded terse, and he reached for hand, but she pulled it hand back. "I'm looking at other options, too, of course," he assured her.

She looked up stubbornly. "Business is improving, you know. A few locals come in for dinner sometimes, and we have a wedding reservation scheduled."

"That's wonderful," he assured her, knowing that one wedding would probably not be enough to save the inn. But for Lindsey's sake, he remained hopeful.

She cocked her head. "Are you always a cheerleader, Donovan?"

"Not always." Donovan admitted. Her heart-shaped face was close, her velvety eyes so deep and inviting he didn't breathe. Lindsey looked mesmerized, too. He had the sudden urge to kiss her, but—

"Mom!" came a loud voice suddenly. Donovan pivoted around to see who was calling her. Leo stood on the stairs with brows furrowed, and one step behind him, Archer leaned against the wall with tousled hair. His eyes were round, and his thumb was inserted into his mouth.

"Hello, boys," chirped Lindsey in an unusually high tone. She brushed past Donovan and hurried to the stairs with her arms outstretched. "Did you have a nice nap?"

"Snacks," commanded Leo in a suspicious tone. Donovan smiled brightly. To his relief, Archer circumvented his twin, thumped down the stairs, and crossed the room. He stopped at Donovan's feet and looked up. Donovan waited for what he expected would be a child's lecture about admiring his mom. The boy pulled his thumb from his mouth. "*Uncah* Don," he greeted him instead. "Up." He raised one arm like a peace offering, and the thumb returned to its favorite place.

Donovan picked up the child and balanced him on his hip. Lindsey held Leo in her arms. "Let's have snacks," she agreed in a singsong voice. She met Donovan's eyes for a split second, then looked away as if disconcerted. Even with his heart racing and his mind spinning, her smooth segue into parenting was not lost on him.

Even though she heard herself speaking, Lindsey's mind was miles away during dinner service. "That chicken smells amazing," declared Aunt Daphne when she swept into the kitchen with the twins in her wake. Archer held a crayon in each hand.

"Thank you for watching the boys." Lindsey wiped the countertop with a soapy sponge.

"I had to get one of the rooms cleaned, but we managed, then took a walk to see Ms. Diane. We're buddies, right?" Aunt Daphne grinned at the boys, the sick day and broken ham platter forgotten.

"I color with Aunt Dappy," chirped Archer sweetly.

"Their plates are over there, *Dappy*," Lindsey pointed out with a giggle. "Yours, too."

"Hot dogs," Leo commanded.

"No, chicken," Lindsey replied in a firm tone. She helped the boys onto the tall chairs pushed up to the counter, and Aunt Daphne took a seat on the other end.

"Aren't you going to eat?" asked her aunt.

"I think I'll eat later." Lindsey wanted to retire to her room and analyze what'd happened with Donovan earlier. She zeroed in on the broom in the corner. "Y'all go ahead, and I'll be right back." She fled to the dining room. It was quieter now with guests dispersed throughout the house. Two sisters from New Jersey were on the back porch enjoying the aftermath of the rainstorm. Daphne had persuaded Isaac to light candles and lanterns before he left for the day, and Lindsey imagined they cast a peaceful glow over the deepening evening accompanied by cricket and frog songs.

She started sweeping with concentrated effort then glanced at the vases of irises resting on the tabletops. The purple-and-white blossoms were lovely. She exhaled deeply before remembering Donovan's long, appreciative look at the kitchen counter. What had *that* been all about? She swallowed uneasily. She hadn't been kissed in a long time. Not since... Her heart thudded. Just being around Donovan made her feel giddy, but she wasn't the type of person to lead someone on. How had a lawyer with his life etched in stone, and who'd already achieved more than she could even dream of, have her in such a tizzy?

She brushed the floor more forcefully. He was an attractive, attentive man. That was all. For a long time now, any thoughts of letting herself feel anything for someone again— or completely trust them—had been tamped down whenever they arose. Just then, a cascade of giggles from the kitchen floated her way, and her heart filled with gratitude for Aunt Daphne. She could have hired a friend of a friend or a local, but she'd taken on her niece and two kids, then pretended Lindsey was the one doing her the favor.

Leaning the broom against the wall, Lindsey put her hands on her hips. The floorboards shined. She had two wonderful boys, her aunt, and parents and a sister who loved her. And just because her husband had chosen to leave her after taking vows didn't mean that someone else would do the same. It was time to stop telling herself she was too busy and too broken to let someone else in. Her heart persuaded her to consider Donovan in more ways than as a guest or a very good friend. She pressed her lips together scanning the clean, empty dining room as her mind rebelled. He was a very ambitious, busy man, and he wanted the inn. Letting herself fall for him was not an option.

Or was he? She just wasn't sure what to do.

Chapter Eight

Donovan set down the last box of his things in the lounge Saturday morning and waited for Lindsey to finish in the kitchen so they could exchange living quarters. The majority of the guests were out and about in town, exploring gift shops and antique stores, and the twins were watching television.

Lindsey seemed in her element at breakfast, as if she'd forgotten all about the tender exchange they'd shared in the kitchen. He'd tried not to think about it, but her soft, gentle movements through the dining room had been a constant reminder.

The charity. The inn. The boys. Donovan walked over and slumped into the comfy couch between the twins. They were mesmerized by the animated animals with first-responder jobs they were watching on TV. He chuckled when Leo laughed, amused by his easy joy. Soon, Lindsey wandered in, smoothing down a pair of black slacks that ended several inches above her ankles. "Are you ready?"

"Sure."

"No," Leo differed.

Donovan laughed again. He slid out from between the boys and stood up. "We'll be right back. You two sit right here."

"Okay, Uncle Don," Leo sang.

"Okay," Archer hummed around his thumb. Donovan grinned at Lindsey, and she shook her head in defeated amusement.

Donovan grabbed his belongings. Then he marched his suitcase and several garment bags up the two flights of stairs, pushing open a door into a narrow room running the length of the house. Shuffling footsteps whispered behind him, and Lindsey caught up. "Every-thing's by the bed," she informed him.

He lugged his stuff into the center of the room and looked around. There was a television on one side, and to his left, a large king-size bed with a frilly canopy. He skirted the boys' toys that were stacked inside of totes and laid his things on the bedspread, trying not to stare at the giant magnolia flowers printed on it.

A burst of giggles made him look around. Lindsey smacked a hand over her mouth. "Sorry," she said.

"No, you're not," he intoned.

"It's not as plain as the cottage, and it has just as much charm."

"Yes, in my grandmother's taste," Donovan returned. He looked up at the lacey canopy. "That's fraying a bit."

Lindsey walked up beside him. "It's tatting. It's supposed to look like that."

"Oh." Donovan smirked. "I don't really mind. I still get my Wi-Fi, a television, and I'm closer to breakfast."

Lindsey chuckled. "And I don't have to worry about the boys jumping up and down and the whole house shaking."

"I'm glad it worked out."

"Me, too. I appreciate it." She smiled. "By the way, I have something for you." Lindsey reached into a folded cardboard box and pulled out Ryan's trophy. "Surprise!" She grinned. "I snuck into the cottage while you were eating breakfast and gathered all the pieces together. I used a special glue that doesn't show and should be pretty sturdy now."

Donovan reached for it, his fingers brushing hers. "Thank you, Lindsey. I don't know what to say."

"I know it means a lot to you."

"It does." Donovan moved to give her a quick embrace but caught himself. He cleared his throat and turned to haul a tote downstairs. "Where did you learn to make cinnamon rolls?" he asked to diffuse the sudden attraction he felt. "You said your mom? Or was it your grandfather?"

"Mom taught me to bake mostly. My grandfather, *Abuelo*, taught me how to cook the good stuff. He was Cuban."

"Wow." Donovan threw a glance over his shoulder to look at her as they rounded the second floor landing. "You must have some great family recipes."

"I do," she agreed. "That roasted chicken last night, for one."

"I liked the citrus seasoning."

"It was my grandfather's special recipe. I adapted a lot of what I grew up eating at home into traditional Southern cuisine."

"Did you ever live in Florida?" Donovan asked. There were so many things he wanted to know about her.

"No, but my mother did as a girl."

"Where are your parents?"

"Still in the Fort Worth area. I lived with them until—" Lindsey broke off, and Donovan pretended to be absorbed by his careful descent down the stairs. "Until I moved here, actually. I lived alone until the boys came along, then moved in with my parents for a while so they could help."

"I'm glad you had somebody."

"Yes, they were great. They wanted me to stay, but I didn't want my problems to be theirs." Donovan raised a brow. She was stubbornly independent, as if she had something to prove. He wondered why.

Side by side, they walked to the cottage, checking on the boys on their way out. "How do you like it here in Kudzu Creek?" Donovan asked.

"I like it a lot. I visited while growing up, but that was before Aunt Daphne and Uncle Jim bought this place. Something about Kudzu Creek always drew me here. Plus, it's closer to Florida than Texas. I have cousins in Miami."

Donovan pushed open the cottage door with his foot and set the toys down. "You're blessed. I only have a couple of cousins, Bradley being one."

"Yes, I finally met him. He was here the other day to spruce up the arbor for Aunt Daphne," Lindsey reminded him. "He's a nice guy."

"He's great." In fact, with Donovan over lunch, Bradley had shared every last little detail about his visit to the Azalea Inn. The twins had hovered around the contractor, mesmerized by his sandpaper and eager to get into the paint. Lindsey had to rescue him twice before suggesting the twins take a walk to Henny House to see what Emily was up to. "He bragged your cookies were the best he'd ever tasted," Donovan informed her. "It made him jealous when I told him I get to eat them whenever I want." That made her laugh. With a lingering grin, she set a box of the twins' clothes on the couch, then sat down beside it. Donovan sat beside her. They stared at the mantel and its knickknacks.

"I really appreciate this, Donovan," Lindsey sighed.

Donovan pretended not to notice how close they were sitting. "I don't mind. It's the least I can do."

"For what?" she teased. "Breakfast? You're so patient with the boys, and giving me this space is going to relieve a lot of stress about annoying the guests."

He smiled, grateful he could make her life easier. "You're amazing. I know I couldn't do it alone." Something in her eyes flickered, and she went rigid. He continued, "Do the boys get to see their birth father much?" Lindsey suddenly folded her arms over herself in a protective motion. "I'm sorry, I don't mean to pry," Donovan backpedaled.

"You're not," she said in a stoic tone. "I can talk about it." Donovan waited. The cottage was silent except for the steady ticking of a brass clock in the other room. "I met Keith when I was in college. He was getting his PhD, and I was finishing a culinary degree after spinning my wheels in different majors over the years. In the meantime, I worked as a sous chef at a nearby restaurant, and I loved it because I always wanted to have my own place someday. We got married and bought a lovely home, but I put off my culinary dreams and ran an orthodontics office instead."

Donovan watched her foot tap the coffee table. "Did you like the office environment? I bet you were great at it."

"Maybe, but not really," she admitted. "I prefer pastries over paperwork, but Keith wanted me at home when he was, which made sense. If I'd continued working at the restaurant, I would have had crazy hours. That's how marriage works, you know. Compromise."

"Of course," Donovan agreed. "What did he give up?"

She shook her head. "Nothing. I soon realized that he wasn't a compromiser. He had important goals, and I made allowances for them." She looked toward the tote of toys. "But I always assumed we'd have children. We talked about a family, but when he received a promotion at NASA, he asked me to hold off having babies. Not long after that, he informed me he didn't want kids and suggested we get a dog instead."

"Did you?" Donovan asked in surprise.

"Yes." She smiled wistfully.

"No wonder the boys love Kessler so much."

"They never met Ursa," Lindsey admitted. "She was a big, slobbery bear. Keith was furious when I found out I was pregnant, and after weeks of arguing, he told me he'd met someone at work and asked me to move out. He wanted the house, and he kept the dog, too."

Donovan tried to hide his amazement.

"I couldn't have afforded the house on my own anyway. So it made sense for me to move out."

"But it still hurt?"

Lindsey laughed sharply. "We parted as friends, but he isn't interested in the boys." Donovan heard the pain in her voice. "He only saw them once after they were born, although he does help with their support. I would never have been able to buy the van and leave my parents' house, much less support the three of us on what the inn can pay me right now." She met Donovan's gaze for a moment, then shifted her eyes away as if the conversation was difficult. "He's set up a college fund for the boys so I won't have to worry about that. I just have to provide them a home and make sure they're fed."

"And love them."

"Yes. They're my whole world." Lindsey drew her knees up to her chest. "I was in panic mode at first, wondering how I would do it all myself. I know they'll need a father someday, but I'm not ready to worry about that right now."

"You're doing a great job with them," Donovan assured her.

"Thanks." She eyed him warily, and he

smiled. He wanted to reach out and touch her cheek, but it wasn't a wise move.

"I always imagined I'd have kids someday, but not until I had my own law office up and running," he admitted aloud.

"And your charity?"

"Yes, that, too. And a house." Donovan hunched his shoulders in a lazy shrug. "I'm really not that great of a babysitter. Emily gets away with a little too much when I'm around. I fell asleep once, and she cut off a chunk of my hair."

Lindsey giggled. "I don't think anyone's ever truly ready. It's a big sacrifice."

"But the good news is you're cooking again," he grinned.

"Yes, I love managing my own kitchen, and it's wonderful that it's not at a giant, crazy restaurant. This place is so homey, so easy and comfortable. I hope to stay for as long as Aunt Daphne will have us." She hesitated, then turned to face him. "If Aunt Daphne and Uncle Jim had lived here when I visited as a girl, I might have never left."

"That would have been nice. We would have met sooner." Too late, Donovan bit his tongue. He couldn't believe he'd said what he'd said and felt his cheeks redden. "I mean… I didn't mean it that way," he stammered. She gave him a penetrating stare, and he squeezed his fists, wondering if she could hear his heart clanging like a fire station bell.

"Are you still looking at other properties for your charity?" Lindsey asked out of the blue. "You're not in league with the bank, making plans for a takeover of the inn, are you?"

Donovan felt like he'd been doused with a bucket of cold water. "No, Lindsey, on my honor, it's just as I told you. I want this place if it goes up for sale, and if not, there are other houses around."

She sucked in a breath of relief. "I'm glad. The plans are all set for the Winthrop wedding, so all we have left to do is wait for the big day. And bake a cake," she added.

"You're doing the cake?" Donovan wasn't surprised.

"Oh, nothing fancy," she assured him. "It's just two three-layer cakes stacked with a simple buttercream frosting and a few floral decorations."

"It sounds pretty," Donovan encouraged her. "If they're happy with it, that might be another source of income for you, because we don't have any wedding bakers in the area." He quickly corrected himself. "That I know of." What did he know about weddings? "I'm not exactly a romantic," he blustered.

"I doubt that." The corner of Lindsey's smile twitched in amusement.

She was right. He *was* a romantic. He'd just spent a lifetime avoiding it. In the weighted silence between them, he shifted his gaze to her deep, dark eyes. She looked up at him as if reading his mind. Donovan felt a match strike inside his heart, and hope flickered like a candle. As if directed by an unseen conductor, he dropped his head, intent on kissing her, but before he could, a loud noise startled him. It was Daphne, standing at the doorway. "The boys are rolling cinnamon rolls down the staircase," she announced in exasperation. "Both of them. There's icing everywhere."

Lindsey jumped up with an exclamation of surprise, but Donovan did not miss the gleam in her aunt's eyes when he met her gaze. He looked away innocently and followed them out the door with a racing heart, chiding himself for what he'd almost done. He couldn't fall in love with a busy mother of two trying to get back on her feet. He couldn't fall for her twins, either. It didn't make sense if he was after the inn. Not even if his heart wanted something more.

* * *

The next day, after church, where the boys had misbehaved and crawled all over her, Lindsey dropped by the cottage to let them run around the backyard while she freshened up. She tried to think about what she'd learned during the service and not how she was certain Donovan had almost kissed her in the cottage yesterday. She needed to deal with it and be firm, but a part of her wasn't sure she wanted to say anything. Reminding herself about the inn's state of affairs, she loaded the twins back into the van with excited cries of *Emiwee!* and they all looked forward to lunch at the Ainsworths'. Claire had babysat the boys several times, and they loved their playtime with Emily in the spacious house. Toys were allowed everywhere. Emily had a cat named Pony, and Leo chanted the strange moniker all the way to their house. The Ainsworths' semi-Victorian home was a lovely shade of vanilla pudding with a dark purple door. Lindsey unbuckled the boys and set them free just as the front door opened and Bradley waved. Emily dashed past his leg to meet the boys on the wide porch steps.

"Leo! Archer!" she cried, clapping her

hands. They scurried inside to play. "Welcome," said Bradley cheerfully.

"Thank you for having me for lunch," Lindsey called.

"Thank you for coming." He smiled.

She breezed through the beautiful entry and stepped into the parlor, sucking in a breath when she saw Donovan with an arm thrown casually across the back of a gray couch. He sat facing the television, which had a baseball game on. His head snapped her direction when she reached the edge of the plush area rug centered in the room.

"Hey there," he said cheerfully, "you made it."

"You heard the boys, I'm sure."

He laughed and motioned for her to take a seat beside him. "Yes, Emily was watching out the window for you." Claire burst out from the kitchen with bowls of chips and pretzels in her hands.

Lindsey eyed the food spread across the low glass coffee table in front of the television. "This looks amazing."

"Oh, it's no big deal. Just some mini sausages, nachos, pizza bites and fruit salad. But I promise you, there is a veggie plate, too," Claire giggled. "Help yourself."

Bradley came in with drinks, and they all settled down to watch the baseball game and eat. It felt like she'd known them forever, Lindsey thought. She forced the events of the previous day to the back of her mind while Donovan gave her a rundown on the statistics of the team. "I don't follow sports much," she admitted.

Donovan promised she'd change her mind if she lived in Kudzu Creek long enough. Lindsay laughed. "Maybe. Plus I do want to put the boys in T-ball next year."

"It's never too early," said Bradley, and his wife rolled her eyes.

"I think I'll just be happy with this delicious dip for now," said Lindsey. "Does it have dill in it?"

"It does," Claire admitted. "There's pie, too, for later."

Lindsey stopped herself from eating any more chips and reached for the plate of veggies instead. Beside her, Donovan leaned in at the same time, and their fingers tangled. "Sorry," she chuckled, trying not to show how much she liked feeling his hand against hers. Sitting beside him felt so normal. She blinked and offered the plate instead. "Celery? Oh, wait, you don't like celery, right?"

"It's just plant thread." Donovan grimaced.

"Carrots, then?"

He winked and took a handful, then reached for the dip. Her cheeks heating a bit, she sat back, eyes riveted on the television as if she worshipped baseball and did not feel Claire and Bradley's gazes on her. Someone hit a ball, and Lindsey cheered like a good guest, while the men jumped to their feet and bellowed. She glanced at Claire with amusement. Claire gave her a small grin and bit into a carrot so hard it snapped. Lindsey pretended not to notice at all.

Donovan followed his cousin into the kitchen to prepare dessert. Bradley opened a cabinet and reached in for a stack of small stoneware plates. Seeing a blueberry pie on the counter, Donovan fetched it to slice up for the others. Bradley passed him a plate, eyeing him for a long moment. Donovan looked down at the serving. "Did I cut it too big?"

"Not for me." Bradley grinned. "What about you?"

"No."

"I meant, are you cutting off more than you can chew?

"What are you talking about?"

"You're finishing each other's sentences, and she knows you well enough not to give you celery."

Donovan shrugged. "She cooks at the inn. So she knows what I like."

His cousin made a noise in his throat. "The boys treat you like family."

"I practically am. We all live at the inn."

"Yes, but—"

"I know what you mean," interrupted Donovan. Avoiding his feelings for Lindsey was hard enough, but there was no fooling his cousin.

"You like her."

"Of course I do."

"No, I mean you *really* like her. You're re-evaluating your life."

A blob of blueberry attached itself to Donovan's finger, and he licked it. "I told you, we're just friends. We live on the same property, is all—which may or may not be a half-way house by the end of the year."

"I hear business is picking up for them."

"Yes, business is good," Donovan admitted in a dour tone.

"I'm happy for them," said his cousin.

"Yes, I have plans for the place, but I'm not a complete monster. I'm not praying for

Daphne to lose everything," Donovan insisted.

"And your long-term goals?"

"What about them?"

"Since you were twelve you've wanted to be a lawyer, to have your own firm and then to settle down and populate the world with little Ainsworths."

"I have the charity to get rolling right now, but that's still the plan—eventually."

Bradley arched a brow at him. "You could always alter your plan, you know."

Donovan's stomach dropped at the thought. "I admit the idea of a starter family isn't as frightening now as it was earlier. It wasn't right of me to think there was something wrong with that. I've changed my mind."

"I think you've changed your mind about a lot of things," Bradley observed.

Donovan shook his head, but it didn't feel as earnest as it should have. "You do realize I'm waiting for her to lose her home so I can take it for myself, don't you?"

"Maybe you need to change your mind about that, too." Bradley took a plate with pie in each hand and walked out. Donovan filled two more plates with blueberry pie. Ryan's House was still going to happen. He was really hoping that he'd be able to buy the inn, but if it didn't work out he'd deal with it. Donovan didn't wish Lindsey or Daphne any ill will. Besides, someone would purchase the Azalea if it went into foreclosure. So why not him? His head started to spin with all of the thoughts and emotions swirling around.

Lindsey and her twins had thrown him for a loop, as his mother would say. He'd never imagined living in an inn, and he'd never thought he wouldn't want to leave. Maybe being a little more flexible was a good thing. Maybe letting life take him where he needed to go without checking his planner every hour would be healthy for him. In the past few months, he'd been more excited about waking up each day, about his cases at work and even about walking Kessler. The world seemed a little more colorful. He felt happier.

Donovan scooped up several plates at once. He couldn't remember the last time he'd enjoyed hanging out at his cousin's so much, and he had the sneaking suspicion he knew exactly why. Maybe for now he could worry about Ryan's House and the inn another day.

Chapter Nine

A few days later, Lindsey packed Leo and Archer into their stroller to have lunch at Southern Fried Kudzu. She'd planned a lighter dinner than usual for the guests—traditional hot chicken-salad casserole with fresh greens on the side—which gave her extra time to spend with the boys. A few minutes into their walk, she spotted Claire pushing Emily toward them in the distance, and they met halfway before walking toward the café.

"Bradley's at a work site today," Claire explained over Emily's jabbering. The boys were silent, Archer listening politely and Leo furrowing his brow while Emily explained how many crayons she had and that no one was to bite them.

Lindsey chuckled. "He minds Emily a lot

during the day? I saw how good he was with her last weekend." Lindsey had admired how Bradley had cuddled with his daughter on his lap and let her eat most of his pie.

"It depends on his schedule," Claire explained. "We've worked out a system that gets him home a couple hours before dinner so I have time in the studio before and after if I need to finish something up."

"And he helps in the kitchen."

"He doesn't mind," promised Claire. "And I appreciate it too much to complain, so I eat what I'm offered. I appreciate you keeping Emily for a couple hours a week, too. She loves playing in the backyard at the inn."

"I'm happy to do it, and the boys love it." Lindsey smiled. Most of her friends in Houston were so busy with their own lives they only contacted her once in a while, and her coworkers at the orthodontist office had faded away after she'd resigned. A few had sent baby gifts, but other than her parents, aunt and the occasional call from her sister on the other side of the country in California, she rarely thought of herself as having anyone. Did mothers have friends? Apparently in Kudzu Creek, they did. A feeling of affection for the town washed over Lindsey.

She'd always liked Georgia, but she realized she was coming to love it.

They finally reached their destination, and Lindsey stepped inside the infamous café. Between newspaper clippings and a few framed photographs on the walls, not to mention fresh white paint with a stenciled green ivy border, it could steal a piece of her heart, too. Her mouth watered as the scents of beef, bacon and onions mingled with fresh bread. The tangy smell of curry made her heart pound with excitement that something special was also on the menu today.

Claire led the way to the counter with Emily on her hip, where Mac greeted them pleasantly. "Hi ladies."

"Have you started the new book for book club yet?" Claire asked.

"I have." Mac smiled. "And I'm really enjoying it. How about you, Lindsey?"

"I like what I've read so far," Lindsey admitted. "I'm not a fast reader because I have to mull everything over."

"I totally understand," chuckled Mac.

Claire beamed. "I've read half, but I forget pretty quickly, so I'll need a refresher before we meet." She put in an order and stepped back. The twins chased Emily around her legs. Lindsey ordered grilled chicken bites and homemade macaroni and cheese for the boys, and when she hesitated at the long list of hamburgers, Mac suggested she try a chickpea-and-rice dish with fried kudzu.

"We have an eclectic menu," Mac said with a grin. Her dark hair gleamed from the loose bun on top of her head. "Half of our customers want traditional diner stuff, but the others like café options with a little more flair."

"Kudzu?" repeated Lindsey. "With rice?"

"It's just a green," laughed Claire. "I don't mind it."

"It's our signature dish," Mac teased.

Lindsey thought that if it wasn't bad, kudzu might be a charming twist to the inn's menu rotation. It would certainly be something to remember. After paying, she herded the twins to a table and strapped each of them into booster seats that Claire had retrieved from a corner of the room. They were just sitting down when Claire turned to Lindsey with a grin. "Well, look who's here."

Lindsey looked around, surprised to see Donovan at the door with an elderly man at his side. The unexpected sight of the lawyer made her heart cartwheel. He wore the same slacks and tie he'd had on that morning, but

the gentleman beside him sported casual kha-
kis and a shirt, with reading glasses hanging
from his neck. Two pens were clipped to his
front pocket.

"He eats here a lot, I understand," Lindsey
recalled. Not appearing to see her, the two
men set their things down on a table by the
window while engaged in conversation. "I'd
say hello, but I shouldn't bother them," Lindsey decided. She shouldn't feel so fluttery
seeing Donovan out and about town when
she'd just seen him that morning.

Claire passed out crayons she'd pulled from
her purse, along with a small notepad. "That's
Judge Sheldon. Have you met him?"

"Don't bite my crayons," Emily reminded
the twins. Lindsey saw that Leo had one in
his mouth. He threw Emily a challenging
stare.

"Leo, don't eat that. Yuck," Lindsey cried
as she pulled it from his mouth.

Claire patted the piece of paper in front of
him. "Draw me a monster," she suggested.
This redirected all of the children's energy.
Lindsey leaned her head back to check on
Donovan and the judge. The older gentleman
was Isaac's grandfather, she remembered. She
should meet him. Giving Claire a small nod,

she stood up and crossed the room. Their heads were bent over their table in concentration. She slowed her steps, worried she might be interrupting something. Donovan looked a little troubled, but before Lindsey could stop, the judge noticed her. Then Donovan saw her and looked alarmed.

"I—" she began, stepping forward. "I'm sorry, I just wanted to say hello," she stammered, feeling flummoxed. Judge Sheldon rose to his feet, and Donovan followed suit. She glanced at the judge. "I'm—"

"This is Lindsey," said Donovan quickly, clearing his throat. "Lindsey Judd," he repeated. He glanced sideways at her. "This is Judge Sheldon."

"Ah," said the judge, not the least bit disconcerted. He held out a hand, and she took it. It felt dry but warm. "Isaac has told me all about you."

"Me?" Lindsey put a hand on her heart. "Oh, I don't know about that. We share lunch sometimes. Talk a little. Aunt Daphne is the one who set it all up." Lindsey nodded toward Donovan. "With Donovan, I mean."

"He fits right in with the inn crowd," joked Donovan. There was something strange about his tone, and Lindsey wondered if she'd done something wrong. They'd watched morning cartoons with the twins yesterday, and he'd told her goodbye, with another wink, before heading off to work this morning. It'd made her heart surge. She wanted to believe he only did it for her, but that would be silly. He was a lawyer, an expert at charming people. She treasured his friendship. He'd become a part of her life in Kudzu Creek, but she had to wonder if they'd ever be anything more to each other. "It's nice to meet you, Judge," she stammered, returning to the man's watchful gaze.

Judge Sheldon reseated himself. "I'd invite you to join us, but it looks like you already have a lunch date."

Lindsey looked over her shoulder as Donovan sat back down, too. The kids were coloring furiously, and Claire was studying her phone. "Yes, the boys are mine. Leo and Archer." The old man's brows rose with amusement.

"Their father was—is—an astronomer," Donovan explained.

That was her cue to return to the table. "I guess I'll see you at dinner?" Lindsey asked Donovan, then her cheeks turned hot when she realized it sounded like she was keeping tabs on him.

"Of course." Donovan smiled, but it didn't reach his eyes. Lindsey glanced at Judge Sheldon. "I didn't mean to intrude."

"You didn't," Judge Sheldon assured her. "We were just talking about the inn."

"Oh?" Curiosity kept Lindsey's feet planted.

"Yes," he went on. "I've always admired that beautiful house. And I was just telling him not to worry about a loan if he buys the place. I'd love to be a partner and own a piece of it, and together, I think we could do cash."

"A partner?" Lindsey felt like she was falling through space. Her mind swam desperately to understand. "The law firm?"

Judge Sheldon smiled. "I meant with the charity. Ryan's House. He wants me to be on the board, and I'd like to help buy the property that will be donated for the use of the halfway house. Zoning won't be a problem with my connections."

Silent, Donovan was focused on the judge as if Lindsey was not standing there. "So, even though we're catching up with the bank, you're still planning to make an offer," Lindsey clarified. She drilled Donovan with a stare. He turned his dark green eyes on her and shrugged.

"I know the inn's on track, and I'm still looking at real estate, but should… Well, I mean—"

"If things don't work out, we want the bank to know we're interested," explained the judge, "and we're going to be ready. We'll take over the inn and make sure it's put to good use."

"Yes, I know the *plan*." Lindsey's stomach roiled. Donovan had admitted to her that he was interested in buying the inn, but why was he moving forward as if he knew it would fail? He'd said he loved it there. Had it just been empty words? Like, "I love you, but I love my life more?" or "I love us, but I love my career best?" He didn't love the Azalea Inn, not if he was seeking a partner with a great deal of influence in town to further his plans.

"It's not going to fail," she said in a confident voice. She kept her tone even, matter-of-fact, but inwardly, she seethed. Obviously, no matter how much he enjoyed the inn, Donovan was not going to change his ambitious, determined mind. He may have been considering other options, but he was still planning to do what he'd always wanted—to own the inn at any cost.

She turned away, unable to look at him. He hadn't laid any plans to rest like she'd assumed. He was still moving forward and hoping for what was best for him. She was surprised that he'd been so supportive about the wedding-venue idea.

Lindsey walked back to the table feeling sick from head to toe. Mac had dropped off their lunches, and the boys were diving into their mac and cheese like they hadn't seen food in a week. She slumped into a chair and looked down at a steaming bowl of golden rice and toasted chickpeas. There were swirls of dark green that looked like spinach.

"Are you okay?" Claire asked with concern.

Lindsey couldn't pretend she was. Betrayal pricked her all over like thumbtacks. She couldn't work in a restaurant right now. She couldn't go back to an office. She should have never trusted Donovan had her best interests at heart.

"Don't worry," Claire comforted her, with no idea of what had just transpired across the room, "kudzu just looks scary. It's actually good for you."

Lindsey picked up her fork and dived into the dish. But she was so numb from the situation with Donovan that she could barely taste the food.

A couple days later, Donovan walked up the driveway of the Azalea Inn with heavy footsteps. A street lamp across the road cast just enough light for him to see the outline of the house, where small solar lanterns lined the sidewalk to the front door like an airport runway. The honeysuckle and petunias along the driveway enticed him to relax, but he couldn't work out an ache between his shoulders. His casework had felt secondary to the odd sense of panic that had weighed on him since his lunch with the judge. Judge Sheldon had just made his offer to help buy the Azalea seconds before walking into Kudzu's, and Donovan barely had time to digest the possibility before the man explained his intentions to Lindsey. Donovan had watched the blood drain from her face, and it'd pierced him like an ice pick.

His messenger bag bumped his leg as he rounded the back of the inn. Soft murmurs told him guests were out on the back porch, and he tried to put a more pleasant expression on his face. Donovan's stomach grumbled. He'd skipped breakfast for two days and missed dinner tonight, too, but he didn't have the courage to walk into the kitchen right now. Lindsey probably thought he never meant a word he said—that he was researching other options. Instead, he looked like a greedy businessman just waiting for her to fail. Frustrated, Donovan walked across the yard to the cottage but stopped when he saw the lights on. Suddenly, he remembered it was no longer his place. He was in the attic suite now. Glancing at his watch, he saw it was the twins' bedtime. Lindsey was probably tucking them in after feeding them dinner and cleaning up the kitchen. Now was not the time to bother her. Besides, he wasn't sure he had the nerve. She'd avoided him for days.

Donovan exhaled and retraced his steps. He felt like a coward returning to the house, but he marched up the stairs after greeting his fellow guests. He plowed inside the suite, clicked on a dim lamp, threw his belongings into the double-wide chair beside the television and plopped down to stare out one of the narrow windows.

The walls felt like they were closing in. Donovan wished Leo or Archer were around.

He loved watching their eyes widen at something new or their unrestrained giggles when they heard something silly. He threw his head back and stared at the ceiling.

Just days ago, Lindsey had sat beside him in the cottage with her leg pressed against his, and it'd felt like they had a special connection. Bradley had been right. Donovan liked her much more than as a neighbor, personal chef or a friend. He forced himself to accept it. He got up from the chair and peered out the window. Kudzu Creek was silent. He had work to finish, but for some reason it felt like a chore instead of something that would bring satisfaction when he completed his tasks.

Suddenly, life outside the office mattered more. More than his current case. More than the acquisition of any property. Even more than the timeline for Ryan's House. He was not a machine, Donovan reminded himself. He'd been privileged to accomplish all his dreams up to this point. So, was the charity really for Ryan? Or was he doing it for another reason?

On a whim, Donovan dug for his phone and flipped through his texts. He'd just passed on an offer from Bradley to take a day off next week to visit a historical home he would be tackling. Seeing his cousin's next reno project would be a great distraction. He gave himself permission to miss a few deadlines.

Hey bro, count me in to visit that home in Leesburg with you, he texted Bradley. Then he hit Send. For some reason, a huge wave of relief washed over him.

It was a start.

Chapter Ten

The following week, Bradley Ainsworth had promised to watch the twins at Henny House so Lindsey could prep for the book club meeting. She woke them early to drive them over there right after breakfast. The guests had enjoyed a French toast casserole, along with strawberry smoothies whipped up in the blender. After dropping the boys off to play with Emily, Lindsey returned to the inn to make sure the macaroons were defrosted and the pimento cheese–and–bacon sandwiches ready. She sliced leftover cantaloupe and sprinkled blueberries over them before setting them out on the dining table closest to the window. Sunshine shined in, and she decided a small vase with some fresh ferns would look beautiful beside the porcelain-tiered service holding the refreshments.

"Lindsey," Aunt Daphne interrupted her contemplation with a thick voice. Lindsey looked over her shoulder in surprise. Her aunt leaned against the doorframe like she was holding the house up.

"What's wrong?" Aunt Daphne had seemed fine at breakfast, chatting with guests and cheerfully laughing.

"You better come with me."

With a glimpse of the hands on the foyer's grandfather clock, Lindsey followed her aunt into the office. Aunt Daphne slipped into her old swivel chair before the computer monitor and motioned for her to come see. "Look at this," she said in a grim voice.

Heart sinking, Lindsey obeyed. Was it another letter from the bank? She'd thought they were doing so well, and there were still a few weeks left before the deadline. The computer screen was opened to the inn's account ledger. Daphne clicked another tab and a financial statement appeared. She pointed at a line, and Lindsey followed her fingertip to the far right column. Four hundred and twenty-eight dollars? She scrunched her head and backtracked to the billing name. "Who's that?"

"I had to research it. It's an art-software program," Aunt Daphne supplied.

Lindsey's mind raced backward over her expenses. "I didn't buy it."

"I know, and neither did I."

Lindsey squinted in confusion. "Who would— Wait, do you think we've been hacked?"

"I'm not sure, but I…" Aunt Daphne exhaled. "Look there." She pointed to the delivery address.

"That's here in Kudzu Creek," said Lindsey.

"Right again," echoed Aunt Daphne. "It's the same address on Isaac's application."

"Isaac?" Lindsey shook her head. *Oh no.* "Isaac wouldn't have done that."

"He has my banking information. My credit card numbers. He'd been helping manage the reservation system, and he had the card I gave him for purchasing business programs." Aunt Daphne ticked off the facts on her fingers.

"So you think he bought things with it?" Lindsey hadn't told Aunt Daphne about her conversation at the café, and Judge Sheldon's desire to help buy the inn for Donovan. She certainly couldn't now, but what if…?

"I don't know," Aunt Daphne said, "but that's a lot of money. I'm trying to make double payments on the mortgage to catch up before June." She exhaled. "I won't get another chance, Lindsey. If we don't pull this wedding off, they're going to foreclose on the inn." Her voice crackled with emotion, and she heaved her elbows up onto the desk and clasped her hands in a tight grip. "I just can't do this," she whispered. "The worrying, the scrambling. It's not fun anymore." Her voice fractured into sobs. "I hate doing this alone. I miss Jim."

Lindsey threw her arms around Aunt Daphne's waist. "You're not alone. Please don't cry," she gulped. "I'm here, the boys are here, and you have your guests. They make you happy."

"Yes, people make me happy," Daphne sniffled. "My friends and family. But it's not the same without Jim." Her confession twisted Lindsey's insides. "I'm glad you're here, Lindsey. And I do love this house. Thank you for sharing it with me. I couldn't do it without you." They embraced until Lindsey had an idea.

"I know how to run an office, Aunt Daphne. Let me help with the record keeping."

"No." She patted Lindsey's shoulder, then wiped her own face. "You have enough to do running the kitchen and raising your boys. I'll figure something out."

"But what about Isaac?"

Aunt Daphne slumped. "I'll have to speak with him. I guess I..." she looked at Lindsey with sorrow weighing down the lines under her eyes, "I guess we'll have to let him go."

"You're right," Lindsay agreed regretfully. This was not the time to have a thief at the Azalea Inn. The brass chime of the inn's front door burst into song. "The book club has arrived," She climbed to her feet. "I better get to the dining room."

"Yes, and remember to sit down and enjoy yourself, too," insisted Aunt Daphne. "We'll worry about all of this later."

Lindsey gave her another squeeze. "Okay." She left the room feeling her renewed hope for the Azalea Inn deflating onto the floorboards.

Donovan enjoyed his morning off with Bradley exploring an old house from the turn of the century in a little town north of Albany, but he received a disturbing phone call after their adventure. He sat in Bradley's office a half hour later trying to understand Isaac's tearful pleas and explanations. The

Azalea Inn had let him go after accusing him of stealing. Lindsey hadn't said a word about it to him at breakfast. To be fair, they'd hardly spoken to each other since she'd seen him with the judge at the café. Whenever he tried to start a conversation, she'd dart off to take care of something with the boys. Worse, his routine of watching cartoons with Leo and Archer before bedtime had suddenly stopped. She'd kept them in the kitchen with her while doing dishes the past few nights.

Donovan sucked in a breath of frustration as he strode home from Bradley's office in the sultry heat, wondering if he should address Isaac's situation or not. At breakfast, he'd overheard Lindsey mention a field trip with the twins to another guest, and he'd thought about it all morning. Curiosity got the best of him, and he strode into the inn, hoping she wasn't still upset that Judge Sheldon wanted to get involved with Ryan's House.

Daphne sat at the counter. She frowned when she looked up, and he wondered if it was time to consider that he'd worn out his welcome. "Is everything okay?"

"I had to let Isaac go."

Donovan glanced toward the dining room, but there were no guests around. "I just heard, and I'm sorry, Daphne. I had no idea this would happen."

She looked over the rims of her glasses with heavy eyes. "Yes. I know, Donovan. I'm aware the house interests you, but I can't imagine you'd intentionally hire someone to steal from me."

"No! I would never do something like that, and yes, he called me, very upset." Donovan began to pace the floor in front of the counter like he was in the courtroom. "I know what happened, and I hope you can remember he's a young man. He just saw it as borrowing."

"My credit card number?" Aunt Daphne retorted.

"He wanted to put a hold on something— reserve a copy of the latest graphics program. I know he had every intention of paying for it himself when they released it. It was a pre-order."

"With *my* account."

"I know how it sounds," Donovan assured her, "but I trust this kid, Daphne. I've known his grandfather my whole life. They're a good family."

"Most families are."

"He just made a mistake," Donovan insisted. "We all do. It was foolish."

"Especially when he's already in trouble."

Ryan's face appeared in Donovan's mind. "Sometimes we don't learn the first time. Or the second. Please don't give up on him."

"I'm not going to press charges," Daphne assured him, "but I have to let him go. It's not that I don't appreciate everything he's done, but I'm not sure I want people in the inn who I can't trust."

Donovan cringed. "You can't give him one more try? Can't you see how hard it is for kids like this to get a second chance?"

Daphne gave him a serious stare. "Business has picked up," she informed him, "and we're doing well, but not enough to pay back what we owe fast enough." She tossed a red pen onto the counter in frustration. "I'm still a little short, and I didn't want to worry Lindsey, but I had to tell her everything. I don't suppose you could talk to some of your contacts and see if we could get another extension?"

Donovan gave her his honest opinion. "They don't usually do that, Daphne. I'm sorry."

"I'd assumed Isaac was keeping you informed, what with your interest and all."

"What? No!" Donovan shook his head in denial. "You had him sign a confidentiality agreement when he was given access to your accounts, and he's honored that. I even talked with him about how important it was." Disappointment washed over Donovan at her subtle accusation. "Did you think I was using him to keep tabs on you?"

"Maybe," she sighed. "I shouldn't have even suspected it, but Lindsey brought it up. I apologize. I know you better than that."

Donovan's chest ached. "Is that what Lindsey believes?"

"She wants to give you the benefit of the doubt, but since we know Judge Sheldon offered to help with the takeover, it doesn't look good." Daphne gave him a hard stare. "She told me about it this morning."

"It's not a takeover," argued Donovan. "I should thank her for the benefit of that doubt, but I don't think she's giving me much."

Aunt Daphne seemed to sense something, and Donovan wondered if his wrestling his feelings for her niece was becoming transparent. "I need to talk to her."

"Now may not be a good time," Daphne warned. "She's a little stressed with the catering for the wedding after Isaac's additional charges."

"She needs a break."

"That's what I told her," agreed Daphne. "In fact, I suggested she take the twins out and get away for a bit. She'd probably getting ready to leave. I'm going to prep the vegetables for tonight."

"That's nice of you." Donovan knew why he'd felt inspired to take the rest of the day off. He needed to see the boys, help Lindsey de-stress and make sure she knew he had nothing to do with Isaac's actions. He wanted her to know he was a morally decent guy even if he wanted something different for the Azalea than she did. "I'm going to take a walk," he faltered.

Aunt Daphne gave him a knowing look, but he only waved and hurried to the lounge to drop off his things in a corner. Three women his mother's age were watching a talk show on the television, and one was giggling hysterically. "Ladies," he returned at their friendly greeting. He strode through the French doors toward the cottage but heard a child's voice and turned to the cars parked at the end of the driveway. Lindsey was strapping one of the twins into the van. Squinting through the bright sunshine, Donovan decided it was Leo. Rolling up his shirtsleeves, he headed toward them.

"Need some help?" He pasted a cheerful grin on his face.

She ducked her head back into the van to buckle Leo. "Uncle Don!" the boy called.

"Hey, Leo. Heading out somewhere?"

Lindsey backed out and brushed a loose strand of hair behind her ear. "We're going for a drive. I need to get away." She wouldn't meet his eyes.

"Is there anything I can do to help?"

"You've done enough."

"With the wedding preparations, I mean," Donovan offered.

"No."

Donovan sighed. "I guess you heard about Isaac."

"Yes."

"I'm disappointed in him," Donovan assured her.

Lindsey put a hand to her hip. "Is that all? He cost Aunt Daphne hundreds of dollars."

Donovan winced. "It was a poor choice. He didn't think it through, but he'll pay her back as soon as he can."

"I guess boys will be boys." She sounded clipped.

"Is that what you expected me to say?" Donovan stirred the gravel with his foot, scrambling for a better rebuttal. Leo kicked the back of the seat in front of him. "Yes, boys are curious and impulsive and not all of us learn to control it before we get into serious trouble."

Lindsey took the hint. "That's what parents are for."

"It takes a village, they say."

"And a charity, I presume." Lindsey slammed the van's door shut. "You know we have this big wedding scheduled. Did you know Aunt Daphne received another email asking about one this fall?"

"That's great news for you," said Donovan, amazed at her faith. "We can talk. Where're you heading?"

"Kudzu Creek."

He furrowed his brow. "Downtown?"

"No," Lindsey elucidated, circling the van to the driver's side, "the actual creek."

"I happen to know a great place," Donovan offered. "The boys could take off their shoes and wade. It's shallow."

"What about your office hours?"

"I decided to take the day off. Bradley and I looked at one of his upcoming projects this morning, and I decided not to clock back in."

"Is that so?" Lindsey seemed impressed as she opened the driver's door.

"Yes, why not? I don't have to be working every second of the day, and Mrs. Lewis has everything under control. I'll get my messages from her this evening."

"Okay, if you want to come along, hop in." The passenger door beside him unlocked with a click and Donovan jumped inside. Lindsey cranked the air conditioning. "So, you're taking the day off to go wading with children?"

"There are more important things than the office," he replied.

Lindsey gave him a suspicious glance. "Where's the real Donovan Ainsworth and what have you done with him?"

Chapter Eleven

"What were you hoping to do at the creek?" Donovan asked as Lindsey steered them toward Kudzu Creek.

"I'm going to pick kudzu. That's what the baskets are for."

"Why are you picking kudzu?"

"I tasted some at Southern Fried Kudzu and liked it," she said. "Despite the fact that it's going to swallow up the world."

He chuckled. "That's an old folktale."

"I don't know much about it."

"Kudzu was imported from Japan," Donovan explained. "It was touted as a decorative solution for soil erosion in the beginning. In the sixties and seventies, it became a scapegoat and symbol of poverty and despair because of its wild growth throughout the South."

"That's kind of sad."

"It ingrained itself into our lives here, so depending on your truth, you see it as friend or foe."

"How do you see it?" Lindsey wondered. Donovan didn't seem the type to like a plant he couldn't control.

"As a friend," he answered. "Kudzu Creek was originally called Allensville. After kudzu made its way through Georgia, the town's name was changed in the forties."

"Interesting."

"Yes," Donovan agreed.

"I think these days most of us think of it as a complex Southern character. It's a part of home, but every home needs improvements at some point."

Lindsey understood. She realized she wasn't doing much to improve the situation between her and the man next to her. It was hard not to keep him at arm's length with the future of the Azalea Inn hanging in the balance. Before she could explain, the GPS instructed her to slow down, and she pulled into a small, pebbled area off the highway "Is this the place?"

Donovan nodded as she eased along a row of parking spots. A brown sign staked in the ground reminded dog owners to keep their pets leashed. They hopped out and opened the door for the boys. Lindsey fetched Archer, and Donovan helped Leo out of his car seat. Hand in hand, the four of them walked under a cool canopy of trees over a narrow dirt path. The boys chattered with excitement as they marched to the edge of the creek. A small waterfall poured over a rock shelf in the middle and formed a wide, shallow pool before funneling away downstream.

"Water," shouted Leo.

Lindsey inhaled the fresh air with delight. "This is beautiful. How did I not know this was here?"

Donovan chuckled. "It's a nice fishing spot. The best thing is it doesn't get too many people because it's not deep enough to be a real swimming hole." Lindsey inspected the flat, sandy shallows as the boys began picking through small rocks at the water's edge. Beyond the small falls, she saw an eroded embankment overtaken by kudzu. "And there we go." She pointed.

"Yes, fresh kudzu," grinned Donovan. "You're not going to put it on the wedding cake, are you?"

"Now, there's an idea," Lindsey chuckled,

"but no, just rose petals and some edible gold flakes."

"Sounds lovely." Donovan shared a story about his favorite birthday, when his mother burned his cake and had to make giant ice cream sundaes instead. "She let me build one as tall as I wanted because she felt bad. We measured it at eleven inches." Lindsey burst into gales of laughter. "Speaking of my mother," Donovan declared, "she asked me to invite you to dinner this Sunday after church."

Lindsey smiled, flattered at the look of eagerness on his face. "She mentioned that at book club, but we never scheduled anything."

"She'd really like you to join us."

"I'd love to," she admitted. She liked Vi a lot, and she liked her son, no matter how much she tried not to. A dinner invitation made Lindsey feel like a real part of Kudzu Creek.

"Mom!" Leo called. He was struggling to remove a stubborn sandal. Lindsey hurried over to help, excited to wade into the creek with the boys and play. They plunged into the shallow water, laughing when Donovan joined them with his pants rolled up to his knees. He twirled Archer in circles just high enough for his toes to skim the surface, and the twin squealed with delight. Afterward, the boys shrieked and laughed until they decided to throw rocks again, and Lindsey seated herself on the bank, while Donovan volunteered to gather a few vines of kudzu. He returned with an armful, and she noticed he was scratching his arms. "Are you sure that's not poison ivy?"

"I think so. I was more worried about snakes than anything else. Kudzu's a great place for them to hang out."

Lindsey shuddered. "I didn't think of that."

He sat down beside her, his neck streaky and red. She widened her eyes in concern. "You might be allergic." Unable to resist, she ran her finger along his throat. Feeling his warm skin made her feel lightheaded.

He caught her hand. "I'm pretty sure I'm not. I've eaten it. It's probably just chiggers."

She let him keep his grip although all logic said she should pull away. "It makes me wonder why we put up with living here. In the South, I mean."

He gave her a faint smile. "It's home."

"I feel like it is," she conceded as her heart stirred at the thought. She checked the boys and saw them wiggling their toes in the mud.

Kudzu Creek did seem like a good fit, but how long would the feeling last?

"Do you miss Texas?" Donovan asked, pulling her from her wistfulness.

"Not much," Lindsey admitted. "It'll always be my first home, but I never felt like it was my forever destination." Peaceful rays of sunshine warmed her shoulders. "Kudzu Creek just feels...right."

Donovan squeezed her fingers, and her heart felt like it was about to burst. "It does."

Disconcerted, Lindsey focused on the distant waterfall and watched the creek leap over its crest, dancing and spinning before it hit the bottom pool. She swung her gaze back to the twins. They needed a home. She needed a career plan. Donovan didn't fit into either one. But...for the first time in ages, she had feelings, and they were building, slow and easy. Much deeper than Kudzu Creek. She slid her hand from his grasp.

"Are you all right?" Donovan's concern melted her resolve to stay strong.

"Yes," she answered in a strangled voice. She cleared her throat. "The boys' birthday is coming up," she divulged. "Working on the wedding cake has me thinking about their cake and..." Lindsey took a deep breath. "I assumed their father would come if I sent an invitation."

Donovan's thumb brushed across the top of her hand, making her stomach flutter. "Have you heard from him?"

"He sent birthday money, but there were no questions or any kind of interest."

"I'm sorry," murmured Donovan. "He doesn't know what he's missing with his head in the stars."

"Mommy, watch!" cried Archer.

Lindsey watched her son throw a pebble as far as his little arm could manage. "Good job!" she called out.

Leo mimicked him and hollered, "Me too! Me too!"

"You, too," she laughed. He reached down for a handful of wet sand and poured it over his brother's head in celebration. Archer squealed.

"Leo, don't," Lindsey warned.

"Don't," Archer repeated with more emphasis.

Donovan restrained a chuckle.

"Don't encourage them," Lindsey whispered. "They enjoy combat as much as they do getting into trouble."

"It makes me wish I had a brother," he admitted.

"You have Bradley."

"Yes," he agreed.

Lindsey wondered about Ryan. "You said Ryan was like a brother to you, too."

Donovan stilled. "We became friends in middle school," he explained in a soft voice. "I didn't have an older brother to warn me what I was getting into, what to wear, how to act…" He grinned at her. "Or how to behave with girls."

"I'm sure you figured that one out for yourself," Lindsey shot back with a smile.

"It took me a while," he admitted. "I was more interested in pleasing my teachers, making the highest grades and being everybody's buddy. Ryan got me into running, and we created our own crowd of friends."

"Then it was on to class president?" Lindsey guessed. When Donovan looked at her curiously, she said, "Claire mentioned it at book club." He shrugged modestly. "Did you date in college?"

"I did. Things just didn't work out. I mean—" Donovan looked at her sheepishly. "I guess *my* head was in the stars. At some point I believed there was no limit to what I could do, and I wanted to achieve everything so I'd have a remarkable resume, and maybe become a district attorney or judge."

"But I'm guessing it cost you some relationships."

Donovan stared out across the water. "Friendships, too. Like Ryan."

"Did he stay in Kudzu Creek?"

"Not exactly." Donovan grew grim. "He stayed around for about a year, and we hung out when I was home on breaks, but he'd started running with a different crowd and staying out all night, doing things he shouldn't. That led to habits which made it hard to keep a job, and then…" He hesitated and stared at the twins. "Then one day he called and asked if he could move in with me. He had nowhere to go because he'd gotten into trouble for stealing money from his parents."

Lindsey let out a quiet gasp.

"Sometimes bad habits become addictions," Donovan explained. "I guess it's not too different from any other obsession."

Lindsey thought comparing substance abuse to ambition was a strange idea, but it was true. "Addiction wears many hats," she mused.

"You're right, and the truth is," Donovan confessed, "I was worried his problems would interfere with my plans. I was going to change the world, but I was really thinking about myself. I let my aspirations get in the way of things that should have mattered more. I told Ryan no, and when I heard he'd moved to Atlanta and found a roommate, I was relieved."

"What happened?" Lindsey asked with apprehension.

"He became homeless." Donovan tapped his chest. "Instead of reaching out to help, I'm embarrassed to admit I was just glad I wasn't in his shoes." He laughed coldly. "It was rotten of me—utterly and completely rotten." Donovan turned to face Lindsey. The regret in his eyes hurt her heart. "I should have tried to help instead of giving up on him like that. I had the resources." He snatched up a rock and threw it so hard up the creek it hit the waterfall. "Instead, I was too worried about my sterling reputation being tarnished."

Lindsey suddenly understood what made the man beside her tick. "That's why this charity means so much to you."

"Yes. I don't want that to happen to anyone else I know. I felt Kudzu Creek deserved to be paid back for what it'd given me, so I opened my own law office here with the intention of doing something for Ryan. It's been my plan since the day of his funeral." Donovan shook his head stiffly. "I can't let him down again."

Lindsey watched his jaw tighten with determination. "What a beautiful way to remember a friend." She touched his shoulder.

"Do you see why it's so important now?" He met her gaze. "Not the inn, but the halfway house? I need to find a special place. I thought the Azalea Inn would be perfect when I heard it was available, but I had nothing to do with what Isaac did. He just made a dumb mistake."

"What about this other property?"

"It's the Blankenship farm. I like it, but it's far from town," admitted Donovan. "I have the paperwork, a grant writer and Judge Sheldon on board. I guess I could go out and have another look at it..."

"I'd be happy to go with you," offered Lindsey.

Donovan shocked her by leaning over and giving her a kiss on the cheek that made her glow inside. "Thank you for understanding."

His green eyes darkened, and he whispered, "You're beautiful, Lindsey." He motioned toward the twins. "You're like a constellation yourself with these two boys. You'll find your way."

She glanced off, not knowing how to respond. Donovan nudged her, and when she looked back, he surprised her by cupping her chin. "A man would have to be deluded to give up someone as special as you," he murmured. Her pulse rocketed, and she let herself swim in his eyes, just for a moment. Donovan brushed a kiss across her mouth that made her heart dissolve like candle wax.

A loud giggle yanked Lindsey back to reality. She pulled away, leaving Donovan's hand in the air where he'd cupped her chin. "I'm sorry," he blurted, I shouldn't have—"

"No," Lindsey murmured. "I mean, yes, you're right, we shouldn't have. My job, my boys. I have a lot going on right now." This was not the time, and certainly not the man. "And you're on a mission," she stammered.

Archer interrupted them by scrambling over the pebbled beach and plopping down soaking wet on her lap. "I'm hungry," he informed everyone. He looked tired, too.

"How about we go find some hamburgers or hot dogs for lunch?" Donovan suggested. His voice sounded strained as if he was just trying to be nice.

From the water, Leo's supersonic hearing heard the one word he loved most. "Hot dogs!" he shouted to the sky with unbridled joy.

For once, Lindsey was thankful for the twins' insatiable appetites because there didn't seem to be a clear path for her and Donovan. And it was breaking her heart a little more and more every day.

After pretending to enjoy a hot dog with Lindsey and the twins, Donovan rode back with them to the inn and escaped upstairs to change out of his rumpled clothes and check his messages. Judge Sheldon had called with news he wanted to discuss in person, and Donovan wondered if it was about the Azalea Inn. He couldn't believe he'd forgotten himself with Lindsey. She'd acted like the kiss was accidental, and it hurt because he could see right through her. He stared at his laptop, heart aching. She was right. Their lives were on different paths.

After skimming through his emails, Donovan returned to his phone messages. He forced himself to listen to the judge's voice mail, and the man's new idea made Donovan scoot to the edge of his chair with interest. Even if the inn met its financial obligations, there wasn't any reason they couldn't still make Daphne an offer. Together, they could make her a generous one she couldn't refuse. It was a good idea. A win-win. Either buy the inn in foreclosure or wave retirement money in front of Daphne's face. But she loved the inn, and Lindsey did, too. Where would Lindsey and the boys go if the inn closed? Were there any other jobs for her in Kudzu Creek?

Tensing, Donovan pulled up the listing of the Blankenship farmhouse. It had potential. It was a good deal. He also had Bradley's contracting skills at his disposal. He could make it work, but he'd have to risk disappointing the judge. Gripping the mouse, Donovan scrolled down the property's stats again. To his shock and disappointment, a bright red flag was superimposed over the picture of the old farmhouse with the word *SOLD*.

What was he going to do now?

Chapter Twelve

With the boys down for naps, Lindsey gathered the ingredients needed for the vanilla cake recipe she was using for the Winthrop wedding, while trying not to dwell on other things. Like her feelings for Donovan. The mixing stand droned steadily as she greased round cake pans. When Daphne came in from the dining room, she murmured, "It smells great in here."

Lindsey agreed. "I had a relaxing day at the creek yesterday, and I'm raring to go." She said nothing about kissing Donovan. That would only put ideas in her aunt's head that would be a waste of time.

"Forty-eight hours and counting till the wedding. Will the cake be okay until Saturday?" Aunt Daphne worried.

"As long as I don't frost it until the day before, the layers will be fine. We'll keep them wrapped tight to prevent drying out."

Aunt Daphne slid onto a stool and rested her chin in her palm. She grinned at Lindsey with anticipation.

"Uncle Jim would be so proud of you," Lindsey murmured.

Her aunt seemed to glow. "You, too. I haven't been able to get this place in order since he passed, but you've helped get things on track. We were just a few thousand dollars short, but with the wedding's down payment and the rest of what we have in the account, I'll be marching out of the bank Monday morning free and clear." She grinned at her big reveal.

"What? How?" Lindsey cried.

Aunt Daphne's smile tightened. "I sold a few things."

Lindsey's elation ebbed. Her gaze went directly to her aunt's empty ring finger. "Please tell me you didn't sell your wedding ring."

"Jim would have been okay with it."

"Oh, Aunt Daphne." Lindsey couldn't believe it. Aunt Daphne had answered her prayers once again, and she'd probably sold a lot more precious jewelry than her wedding rings.

"Thanks to you, I feel like I can breathe again," Aunt Daphne said in a hushed tone.

"Me, too," Lindsey admitted, "but I wish you wouldn't have felt like you had to do that." A timer went off, and she slowed the mixer's speed to a crawl. She was smiling so hard her cheeks ached.

"I wanted to."

Lindsey gave her aunt a long, tight hug. "Thank you for all you've done for us. I am so happy for you."

Daphne pointed at the baby monitor. "I can't believe they're going to be four. Their language skills have improved so much, haven't they?"

"Yes, thanks to Emily," chuckled Lindsey.

"And Donovan," grinned Daphne. "Yesterday, I heard Leo shout, 'Order in the court!' when Archer sat on his fire truck."

"They pick up on things," Lindsey muttered. She wondered what Donovan would do when he heard the wedding event would catch them up with the bank. She felt like dancing. Turning off the mixer, she raised it so the beaters could drip. The batter was a lovely pure white. "This is going to be a good cake," she predicted, not wanting to think about the man who had changed her mind about lawyers—and afternoons lazing on creek banks.

"The arbor and potted plants are all arranged, and the chairs will be delivered tomorrow," Aunt Daphne informed her. She reached for a cake beater as Lindsey detached them. "The back porch is swept and ready for the musicians to set up, and the Willow Room has been turned into a bridal suite. Madison Farrow will love it."

Lindsey gave a thumbs-up. "I'm sure she will. So they reserved the whole second floor?"

"Pretty much the entire property except for the cottage and attic suite," Aunt Daphne confirmed. "The Richardsons check out tomorrow morning, and the Winthrops will have the inn Friday through Saturday night. So Monday's going to be a long day," she warned with a happy laugh, "with a trip to the bank and lots of cleaning."

"That's okay. We'll rest later." Lindsey took a steadying breath, then blurted, "Donovan invited me and the twins to dinner at his mother's house Sunday afternoon."

"Did he? That's lovely," Aunt Daphne responded, while studying her.

Lindsey tried to reign in her anxiety. "I was surprised it was only me and the twins."

Aunt Daphne lifted her brows over the frames of her glasses. "Why are you surprised? How was the trip to the creek?" She reached out for the other cake beater, unashamed she'd already licked one clean. "I was surprised Donovan came home early and went with you, but I'm happy about it."

"You're *happy* about it?"

"It's about time, Lindsey."

Lindsey felt a flush work its way down to her shoulders. Her mind raced for excuses. Yes, she liked Donovan a lot. She wanted to be around him. He comforted her. He relaxed her. She also thought of him as more than a friend, even though she knew nothing could come of it.

"What happened?" Aunt Daphne narrowed her eyes.

Lindsey swallowed down a lump of embarrassment. "We kissed."

"And now you're scared?"

Lindsey turned on the tap at the sink. "I've moved on, Aunt Daphne. I've healed. I'm just not sure I'm ready for a new relationship. I've dated a little, but…"

"But not someone like Donovan."

"Not someone like him," she agreed. "We're just friends, and I don't think the boys and I are what Donovan has in mind for his future. He has ambitions, you know, and I have my own plans, too."

"You can each have your own dreams. It doesn't mean you can't have something wonderful together. You just have to commit to each other."

Rinsing out a few measuring cups, Lindsey let her mind wander for a moment. Falling for Donovan was scary enough, but the thought of giving a serious relationship with him a chance was paralyzing. "I think I'd prefer to let things carry on as they are."

"Are you sure it's not because you don't want to make a decision? That you're afraid it'll be the wrong one?"

"Maybe." Lindsey's eyes stung, and she fought the knot in her throat, thankful her aunt couldn't see her face. "I went all-in with my heart once, and it was a mistake. Besides, I'm not sure other people commit as deeply as I do."

"It wasn't a mistake, Lindsey," Aunt Daphne reprimanded her. "We're supposed to have a partner at our side. It's what God wants for us.

Look how He rewarded you with two beautiful little spirits."

A tear suddenly raced down Lindsey's cheek. She swiped at it with a soapy hand, then jumped when her aunt came up behind her and wrapped her arms around her.

"No relationship is perfect, and no marriage, either," Aunt Daphne whispered. "Even the ones that last have valleys now and then, but it all comes down to staying devoted to the goals of becoming a forever family."

"I just need to find the courage to set that goal again." Lindsey thought of Donovan's planner, and a smile tweaked her cheek. "I guess it's time to open my heart," she admitted, "and quit being scared of getting burned."

"Even a scorched cake can be salvaged," Aunt Daphne observed.

Lindsey chuckled. "With lots of icing." She looked over Aunt Daphne's shoulder at the shining cake pans. "This is going to be the sweetest wedding ever. I'm glad to be a part of making someone's day special."

"A celebration of a new family and a new life," chimed in Aunt Daphne. Her gazed roved around the kitchen at the fine work Uncle Jim had done, and she stuck her hands on her hips. "For all of us."

* * *

Twenty-four hours to go. Donovan read the sticky note Daphne had left on his bedroom door at some point on Friday before dawn. Her excitement was contagious. The air smelled like a bakery as he walked downstairs. He would be thirty minutes late to the office, but he'd texted Mrs. Lewis to let her know not to worry.

The house had buzzed with excitement as most of the guests checked out yesterday afternoon, and Daphne had attacked room after room with her cleaning supplies while Lindsey warmed up a light dinner. Donovan volunteered to play with the twins to keep them busy, and when Archer leaned against his shoulder and yawned, Lindsey helped him carry them both out to the cottage and tuck them in.

He liked putting the boys to bed together. It was a beautiful night, but he stopped himself from asking her to sit on the back porch with him. They'd avoided talking about the kiss since deciding it was a mistake, but an unspoken question hung in the air between them. They'd spent nearly every day with each other since he'd checked into the Azalea Inn—talking, listening, laughing, helping and comforting one another, when they weren't debating the outcome of the inn. Regardless of what she'd declared at the creek, this was much more than friendship. He knew it and so did his heart. But did she?

The twins were in the hallway of the second floor playing, as Donovan went downstairs. He crouched and tousled Leo's hair. "What are you doing up here today?"

"Cars." Leo held up a small plastic car he'd been rolling along the baseboard.

"Mommy said no," Archer reminded him.

Donovan chuckled. "Don't worry, everyone's gone home. I'll tell Mommy it's okay." The boys were not supposed to be upstairs anymore, but he didn't mind them coming to visit him in the mornings. He didn't have that much that could be destroyed except the trophy. Lindsey had set it on the windowsill, and he'd left it there as a reminder to put others' needs before his own desires. He hurried down to the dining room, assuming the twins had already eaten breakfast. He could hear a children's TV show playing on the television in the lounge and considered turning it off, but there weren't any guests to disturb except him, and he didn't feel like a visitor here. He felt at home.

In the dining room, he found Daphne seated at the table closest to the kitchen. There were two containers of dry cereal and a pitcher of milk on the table along with bowls and flatware. "Cereal, it is," he called cheerfully.

She wagged a finger at him. "Lindsey's too busy right now to make anything."

He smiled. "It's going to be hot today anyway, and cereal sounds perfect."

Daphne scooped up some bran flakes and raisins. "I'm glad you approve. She's getting ready to frost that cake and is a bundle of nerves."

Donovan put a hand on Daphne's arm. "How are you? I'm glad to see you took a break to eat something."

"I need to get outside to meet the event company. They're going to set up the chairs we rented."

"Exciting. Is there anything I can do to help?" Donovan asked.

"Don't you need to get to the office?"

"I guess," he sighed, "but I'm already late." The rebellious thought surprised him.

"By the way, I called Isaac last night," he confessed. "He's really embarrassed about what happened and would do anything for another chance."

"I don't know, Donovan." Daphne looked hesitant.

"He knows it was wrong to use your credit card number, but in his mind it was only to reserve his copy. He never meant for the purchase to go through on your account."

Daphne pressed her lips together and tapped her toe beneath the table. "I'll have to think it over. You said there's other community service he can do?"

"Yes, but he wants to be here. He loves the Azalea Inn." Donovan looked around at the cozy dining room. There were boxes of ribbons and flowers stacked on the other tables. "It looks like you could use an extra hand."

"I'll worry about that after the wedding," Daphne informed him, "and by the way, I'm making a full payment to the bank next week." She gave him a toothy grin. "I'll have the rest of the money I need to make things right."

The air in the room seemed to evaporate, rendering Donovan speechless. He realized he was staring blankly at his cereal bowl, listening to Lindsey moving around in the kitchen. "Congratulations." He glanced at Daphne and tried to smile to cover the awkward moment. "Let me get your dishes," he offered, determined to see her niece before he left for the office. Had she known the inn was saved and still rejected him after the kiss? His heart shrank at the thought. She really did have nothing but her twins and dreams of being a chef in her head. There was no room for him. That much was obvious.

"I'm right behind you," Daphne echoed. She picked up a box and followed him into the kitchen. He tried not to show his disappointment. He needed privacy for a long talk about the inn's future and to confront the woman he was falling for.

Lindsey stood at the sink, peering out the window, and his breakfast flopped around in his stomach when he noticed how beautiful she looked in her joggers. "The van is here from the rental company," she announced.

"Oh! On my way," Daphne said in excitement. She hurried out the back door, letting the screen door shut with a smack.

Lindsey leaned closer to the window. "Oh no! Those are metal chairs," she cried. "We ordered white wooden foldouts."

Donovan touched her shoulder. "Let Daphne deal with it. You have the cake to worry about." He set the dishes into the sink and opened the commercial-grade dish-washer. "I'll get these."

"Thank you." Lindsey breathed a sigh of relief. "I hope it's not going to get too crazy this morning, but it has to be white chairs. They're going to have to come back tonight."

Donovan glanced over his shoulder at her as he ran water over the dirty spoons. "Did you get the cake done?" It was nowhere in sight.

She grinned. "Yes, I was up before the sun-rise. It's frosted and looks amazing. I just have a few last-minute things to do, like add the fresh flowers."

"You've hidden it?"

"I can't risk it getting smashed," she ex-plained, "not with trouble lurking around in little sandals. It's in the fridge. We moved everything out of the way and even used the freezer to clear space for it."

"Can I have a peek?"

Donovan followed her to the built-in fridge where she slid open the door on the widest side. A beautiful two-tier cake sat in the mid-dle of a shelf.

"That's really cool-looking."

"It's simple, but—" She reached in and slid it out carefully, treading across the room with light steps to set it on the island counter. "See here?" she asked. She turned the cake stand slightly. "Roses will encircle this layer. It'll be elegant."

"Yes." Donovan stared at her beautiful profile until she turned to look at him. "Simple but elegant," he repeated. The noise of chairs clattering to the blacktop outside became deafening, but he tried to shut it out. "Lindsey," he began after gulping a nervous breath, "Daphne told me she's going to be caught up with the bank. And I—"

She took a step back. "What's that?" They both looked up at the ceiling.

"What?" Donovan tried to hide his exasperation. For once, neither the twins nor her aunt had walked in on them. Everyone was busy. It was the perfect opportunity to tell her everything.

"That noise?" she repeated, looking puzzled.

Donovan listened, but didn't hear anything. "Maybe it's just the air conditioner," he assured her, glancing toward the back door. "Or your fridge?" Her gaze shifted to the back staircase as if she couldn't bear to look him in the eyes. "Look, I'm not upset," he began. "I wish you well, but I was wondering if you've ever thought of…" He stammered to a stop, unsteady from the sprinting pace of his heart. "I appreciate all you've done for me," he managed to continue, "talking, laughing, making sure I'm comfortable, going with me over to Bradley and Claire's house, and letting me hang out with the boys."

"Letting you?" Lindsey repeated. "Donovan, I appreciate all *you've* done." She took a small breath. "I know how busy you are. I know you have your life's plans and the charity," she added. "I'm sorry the property out of town sold."

"You knew?" Something hammered Donovan in the chest.

"I saw it on the website. You didn't mention anything, so I assumed someone else bought it."

"I guess you wanted to make sure the inn was safe from me."

"No, it's not that at all," she assured him, but the words rang empty. "We have this wedding to put on, and because of it, things have turned around. I wanted to see if you'd moved forward with an alternative to the Azalea because Aunt Daphne told me that she'd worked things out."

Donovan searched her eyes, but Lindsey

stepped back leaving a gap between them. "Thank you for all you've done, Donovan. I know you have lots of ambitions, and I respect that. I hope you'll respect mine as well."

They stared at one another while Donovan's mind whirled. "I have no choice but to forget about buying the inn, but should I forget about what happened at the creek? How good we are together? The feelings that I have?"

Lindsey's face reddened. "I have my boys to think about," she whispered. "My own plans."

"And you don't want someone to get in the way of them?" Donovan said. "Or you're just not willing to trust anyone with them again?" Lindsey turned to the cake and began wiping nonexistent crumbs off the platter.

"I knew I shouldn't have gotten distracted from what the charity needed," he said bitterly. A thick drop of water splashed on his nose. Donovan jerked in surprise. He looked at Lindsey in confusion, but she was gazing upward, her jaw slack and lips forming a small O. Another drop hit him on the head. He followed her gaze and saw an enormous circle of water staining the plaster on the ceiling. Water pooled in the center, and a wet stalactite formed. It stretched as gravity pulled on it until it dripped to his shoulder.

Donovan stepped aside of the leak. In the silence, he heard the steady whooshing sound again and suddenly knew what it was. "I don't think that's the air conditioner," he said with dread, and Lindsey cut him off with an "Oh no!" She darted out the kitchen, and he took off after her, almost skidding around the corner of the door. "Oh no, please no!" Lindsey shouted.

The boys! Donovan thought in horror. He'd left them alone on the landing. Daphne had been cleaning all morning, and the rooms were unlocked. He didn't need to be a rocket scientist to guess what had happened. He ran through a puddle and looked down in shock at his wet feet. Water was pouring down a wall of the dining room, creating a river across the floor. He frog-hopped across it and turned the corner to find the foyer two inches deep from a waterfall cascading down the staircase. Lindsey was already halfway up the stairs, slogging against the current.

Then Donovan realized the twins could be in danger. With a sharp burst of speed, he hurdled the steps two at a time and shot past Lindsey on the landing. "Leo," she called from behind him, breathless. Water streamed over the second floor landing through spindles of the banister. Donovan raced through it and headed for the suite over the kitchen's side of the house. He heard, "Mom!" and sprinted through the bedroom door to find a flood pouring out of a bathroom. The twins were standing on a canopied bed, each holding on to a post, staring at the pond around them in fascination.

"Boys!" Lindsey cried. The despair in her voice sent a shiver down Donovan's spine.

"Waterfall," wailed Archer.

"There's a creek," Leo pointed.

Lindsey pounced onto the bed, and Donovan shot into the bathroom where his eyes widened in shock. Both of the sink's faucets were on, and the basin was running over. The bathtub was full and lapping over the sides. Donovan fumbled with the handles of the sink, but they just spun in circles. A strangled cry from the bathroom door made him look back helplessly. Lindsey's face was as white as flour. Her chest heaved up and down like the world had just split in half, but the only explosion was the twins' wailing at their mother's despair. "The inn!" she gasped with a choking sound, then clutched at her heart. "The wedding!"

Donovan jerked his gaze back to the deep pool that had once been a bathroom floor. Underneath them was the kitchen—which would soon be ruined—along with everything else on the first floor of the Azalea Inn.

Chapter Thirteen

Lindsey felt paralyzed. All she could do was watch Donovan scuffle with a plumbing valve under the sink. The boys were safe on the top of the bed, and she realized they could have been seriously hurt or worse. Some mother she was. She put her hands over her face and smothered a sob as water climbed up her ankles. She felt lightheaded until she heard her Aunt Daphne's voice.

"Leo! Archer!" Aunt Daphne had reached the second floor. The boys began to cry louder. Lindsey began to cry, too. Splashing up to the bathroom door, the look on her aunt's face said everything with ominous clarity. "My house!" she moaned. Donovan gave up trying to shut off the water and splashed past Lindsey to calm Archer's high-pitched wailing. Lindsey picked up Leo and waded into the hall. She stumbled down the back staircase to the kitchen, nearly slipping and dropping Leo when she reached the bottom. He slid from her arms as the blood drained from her head, making her dizzy. The ceiling was sprinkling like a carwash, and the Winthrop wedding cake, or what was left of it, had dissolved into a mound on the kitchen island. Icing trickled over the sides of the counter like snowmelt and splashed onto the floor. It made a little river of cake crumbs and bathwater that ran merrily toward the back door. A clump of ceiling plaster fell to the floor with a plop. Leo looked up speechless, and Lindsey snatched his hand and led him outside past the useless, rented office chairs to the cottage. She slammed the door behind her.

The wedding was off. The inn was ruined. The last payment to the bank was impossible now. She squeezed her eyes shut. There was no way she or her boys would ever be welcome at the Azalea Inn—if it remained open. Donovan would have his charity house after all, and she would be homeless again.

"You might as well put a For Sale sign in the front yard right now," muttered Donovan on Saturday night. He slouched over the table in Bradley's kitchen. His cousin carried over a plate of beans and cornbread from the stove and set them down. "I know it looks bad, but—"

"It is bad. It's horrific."

"What's wrong, Uncle Don?" asked Emily from her side of the banquette. She was on her knees, with her hands on the table, completely ignoring her lunch.

Donovan gave her a faint smile. "Nothing, I'm fine, Em. Uncle Don is going to be okay."

"You will be," Bradley agreed, slipping down beside him.

Donovan had told him about the kiss at the creek and then the cold shoulder he'd received in the kitchen before the great tsunami. He passed Emily a biscuit to eat, then reached for the pitcher of milk in front of him. It was in a delightful cornflower-blue vase with a rounded lip. Claire's work, no doubt. "The bride showed up as we were pulling rugs into the front yard, and she had a complete meltdown."

Bradley guessed the obvious. "I assume Daphne had to cancel."

"Yes. The rental company sent the wrong

chairs, the cake was ruined and the house was a swimming pool."

Bradley wagged his head with sympathy. "That's terrible. I guess that means a refund, too."

"Yes, and to top it off, Daphne had to cancel all of her future reservations for the month. It'll take a lot longer than that to get the place cleaned up."

"When's the bank's final deadline?"

"Two days. They'll never make it." Donovan put his elbows on the table and rubbed his face.

"I'm really sorry," sympathized Bradley. "It's awful news for them unless the insurance company comes through quickly and generously."

Things were even worse than Donovan let on. Daphne had looked angry all day and didn't cool down until evening. Lindsey had walked around in a complete state of shock, with a twin hanging on either leg. She'd called Claire, and she'd hurried over to pick up the boys to babysit. The twins began to howl, making tears drip out the corners of Lindsey's eyes. Donovan had wanted to hold her tight in the middle of the front yard until she calmed down, but he didn't have the nerve.

Her life was upside down. Again. And somehow it felt like it was all his fault.

"There's not going to be enough for the late payments." The bank had been more than fair, and with the deadline looming, the property would go into foreclosure at any time. He knew it. Lindsey knew it. Everyone else would know it, and he would eventually make the highest bid. He was Donovan Ainsworth. That's what he did. He won. His gut clenched just thinking about it.

Bradley put a hand on his shoulder. "At least they've had your support. Maybe you can help them find a new place."

The thought of Lindsey and the boys someplace else didn't feel right. Donovan couldn't imagine the laughing, curious, loving twins anywhere else. The cottage was their sanctuary. The backyard was their kingdom. The house was their castle. He exhaled heavily and thought about Ryan and their boyhood fun. "They're supposed to come to dinner at Mom's tomorrow. Lindsey and I could talk then, but what's the point," he wondered in misery. "She's never really trusted me," he told Bradley, "not completely, and I deserve more than that."

"It takes some people longer than others to trust," said Bradley.

Donovan turned his glass of milk around and around with his fingertips. "And how long until she doesn't resent me for buying her inn?"

Sunday morning, Lindsey fixated on the cottage ceiling from the pullout couch while the twins crawled all over her. Sunbeams shifted in and out of the room as clouds sped past the window. She pulled the blanket over her head and curled into a ball. She didn't have the heart to go to church today. Everyone would be talking about the flood at the Azalea.

"Mom," Leo demanded, and she squeezed her eyes shut. There was fruit on the small dinette if they got hungry enough. Her mind drifted from memory to memory in a hazy fog. She'd been blessed with a good childhood and kind parents. She'd survived high school. Things were supposed to be wonderful after having babies, not worse. Life was supposed to be hills and valleys, not canyon after canyon after canyon.

Her stomach twisted with a bitter hunger that wasn't about food. If only she still had a home of her own. If only she had a restaurant or diner where she was her own boss. Her eyes pooled. If only when she stood up for herself, she didn't get her legs kicked out from under her. If only she didn't have to do this alone. She blinked tears away. She'd cried a river of if-onlys the night before. She'd have to live with the hollow hole in her chest for now.

An uneven chair across the room rattled, and she listened to one of the boys crawl up to the table. All of the bananas would be peeled and the apples bitten into once by the time she climbed out of bed and quit feeling sorry for herself. But how could she? The inn was heavily damaged. Reservations were canceled. The perfect job running her own kitchen was over. She thought Kudzu Creek had been the answer to her prayers, and she'd begun to believe it was what she wanted and deserved. Then, there was Donovan. She squeezed her eyes again to disappear, but a knock at the door startled her. Lindsey bolted upright, smoothing her hair while searching the window for the sun's position. The boys had returned to their room, giggling and teasing one another in their own special language.

Lindsey inched to the small kitchen window

and peeked outside. Aunt Daphne was at the door. Lindsey's stomach rolled although a part of her was relieved. At least it wasn't Donovan. She couldn't face him right now. Not his pity, nor the fact his noble dream would be a reality, while hers was in ashes. She pulled the door open just as Aunt Daphne knocked again.

"I wanted to make sure you weren't out in this weather."

Lindsey skimmed the horizon over the house just as a blustery breeze shook the treetops. "Storm's coming."

"Yes, rain from the Gulf. A couple of days' worth, they say."

"Just what we need," muttered Lindsey, "more water." She backed away so her aunt could come inside.

Aunt Daphne didn't acknowledge the unfortunate timing of the weather. She glanced toward the twins' bedroom, then walked over and dropped onto the opened sofa. "I'm surprised you don't sleep in there with the boys."

Lindsey shrugged. "I like them to have their space."

"You've sacrificed a lot." Aunt Daphne's words sounded hollow.

Lindsey slumped beside her. "I know I've said I'm sorry a thousand times, but—"

"Don't. I didn't mean to be so prickly yesterday. It's a disaster, yes, but it's not your fault."

Lindsey hung her head. "Yes, it is. I knew the boys were in the house, but I wasn't watching them."

"It's a team sport," replied Aunt Daphne, "that's what we agreed on. Besides, I was the one who left the door open to the room after I cleaned it." She rubbed her forehead. "When I heard Donovan come downstairs, I assumed he'd check on them and take care of anything if they were in trouble."

"I should have listened better," Lindsey mumbled. "I was admiring the cake." Her mind felt like it was floating in another dimension. Maybe she could sell a few desserts locally to help with payments, or find an apartment and a roommate who liked kids.

"You were finishing a beautiful wedding cake. Any little boy is mischievous enough without eyes on them 24/7." Aunt Daphne folded her hands in her lap.

Lindsey couldn't help but stare at her aunt's empty ring finger. "Do you think we can get another extension?" she pleaded. "I can bake full time. I'll find a childcare center for the twins and contact their father for assistance."

"No." Aunt Daphne sighed. "That's why I'm here. You were missed at church." She slanted her head. "Ms. Olivia wanted to know where the twins and the baker were, and Vi asked about you. You have that invitation to dinner at her house."

Lindsey looked down at her shorts and T-shirt. "Obviously, we're going to miss it. I'll text her. I can't go with the mess in the house.

"That's what I wanted to talk to you about. I stayed up late last night and moved the furniture around downstairs," said Aunt Daphne. "The insurance company will have an emergency cleanup crew here this afternoon."

"Well, that's something."

Aunt Daphne nodded. "I'm going to go to my friend's in Albany for a few days. I have some thinking to do."

"About the inn?" surmised Lindsey with a fresh wave of stomach pain. A loud thump came from the boys' room, signaling they'd turned over their toy box. She winced.

"Yes. Lindsey, I… I'm sorry, but I don't think having the boys here was the best idea after all." The words jabbed Lindsey's heart, and she put her fingertips to her temples. Aunt Daphne patted her leg. "I wouldn't have minded if you were just living here, but working in the kitchen makes it impossible for you to keep an eye on them when I can't."

Lindsey's heart sank like a grindstone. She was being asked to leave. Again. She fought the fist of pain in her chest and tried to be brave. "I understand," she croaked.

"I don't have any answers, and the truth is, I'm tired." Aunt Daphne folded her arms across her lap. "Don't get me wrong. Having you here has been wonderful, but it's just not working. I realized last night I miss Jim more than I love this business. That's why I sold my jewelry—for him, for his inn—if that makes sense."

"It does." Lindsey's eyes misted over. Silence fell over them, heavy and sad. "So you're going to turn it over to the bank?"

Aunt Daphne sighed. "I don't have a choice. I could probably wiggle my way into some other plan to put things off, but I think this is a sign. It's time to shut the doors and save what precious memories I have. The Azalea Inn is through."

Lindsey blinked a rogue tear away. Her aunt put a hand on her knee. "You can stay here in the cottage for a couple more weeks. After cleanup in the house is finished, I'll have the place locked up."

"Will you come back from Albany?"

"Oh yes," Aunt Daphne assured her. "I'll rent a modest home somewhere around here, preferably a smaller one with no yardwork."

Lindsey tried to manage a polite smile as her mind stumbled along. She could not bear to ask to live with Aunt Daphne again. "I'll call my parents today. Mom's been asking to see the boys and wondering when I'm going to visit."

"So, do you think you'll go home for good then?"

Home? Kudzu Creek was supposed to be home, Lindsey thought. "I don't want to, but I can get my old job back at the orthodontics' office. And Dad will love playing with the boys." She knew she was trying to convince herself and swiped angrily at another tear.

Aunt Daphne pulled her in for a long hug. "I was hoping you could find a place here."

"I need some time to sort things out," Lindsey choked.

Her aunt groaned quietly. "Trials do not last forever, Lindsey. You're a tough, smart girl. You'll have a place of your own and a great job before you know it. Remember, God always has a plan."

Lindsey felt numb. "I thought this *was* the

plan. It felt right." *So does Donovan*, something whispered in her head. Had she made a mistake putting him off, pushing him away? "Where's Donovan?"

He took a load of things to his parents' house last night. The renovations on the family guesthouse are finished. He's moving back in."

"That's nice. I know he likes it out there." Lindsey sat back, drained, empty.

Donovan had picked up the boys from Claire's Friday night and brought them home. Before he left with a hesitant, searching look, he reminded her about Sunday dinner at his mother's home. She hadn't responded. What could she say? She had things to do. Plans to make. Disasters to clean up. And there were the apologies. The poor bride and groom had to postpone their wedding plans again. Lindsey closed her eyes. It was better this way. God was shutting another door, and there was no use wondering if Kudzu Creek's lawyer would stay in her life. With his office flourishing and the opportunity to buy the Azalea Inn, he would be moving on, too.

Ignoring the rambunctious noises coming from the bedroom, Lindsey informed her aunt that she'd be gone before the end of the month. After Daphne left, she looked around the cottage stuffed with toys, clothes and baking supplies, and decided the little room wouldn't be missed as much as the inn. When she thought of putting her first chef's kitchen in the taillights and saying goodbye to the man who'd made her believe in possibilities, Lindsey wanted to sink down to the ground and cry another river.

Donovan waited anxiously until half past the appointed hour for Sunday dinner, then gave up his pacing and walked morosely back into the house.

"She didn't change her mind?" guessed his dad. Harold Ainsworth gave him a sad smile.

Donovan flopped down into his seat at the table across from Bradley and Claire. "I texted. I called. She's not answering her phone right now."

"They have a big mess to clean up over there," his mother reminded him. "She's just distracted with the boys and all."

Donovan dropped his hands on the table. "I told her we could keep them again today, but she refused." He'd wanted Lindsey to see where he'd grown up and to meet his father. He'd wanted her to spend some time with his

family the way she'd shared her little family
with him. His mother placed a large pan of
lasagna on the table. It looked delicious, but
he had no appetite. He scooted back his chair.
"I'm sorry. I just can't eat right now." Silence
dropped across the table.

"I'll eat," Emily cried out with the confi-
dence of a four-year-old. The adults chuckled in anxious tones. Not wanting to ruin
things, Donovan left them to enjoy the meal.
He checked his phone again as he passed
through the living room and its great river-
rock hearth, then slid open French doors to
the back deck. There he resumed the pacing he'd begun in the driveway. The afternoon sun ducked in and out of cloud cover.
The air sagged with humidity, and he pushed
his sleeves up. Donovan had decided not to
change out of the slacks he'd worn to church.
He'd wanted to look nice, he admitted. For
Lindsey. He'd wanted her to love his mother's cooking and have the opportunity to be
served instead of doing everything herself—
to sit down and relax and not worry about
the boys.

Leo and Archer. The mischievous twins.
They'd been running back and forth on the
second floor on his way down the stairs Fri-

day morning. Donovan should have mentioned it to Lindsey, or better yet, brought them down with him. His heart felt like a cinder block. He'd been so distracted by thoughts of their mother and his feelings for her, he'd ignored any trouble the boys might get into. He was filled with disappointment. Definitely proof he was not fatherhood material. This was not like Emily painting the cat. The boys could have been seriously hurt or worse if electricity had been involved. What if one of them had decided to climb into the overflowing bathtub? His heart tripped with alarm at the thought, and he put a hand to his chest to calm himself. Memories of Ryan flooded over him. He'd been too distracted to help Ryan, and he needed a lifetime to make it up to him. He wouldn't be able to draw another breath if he'd been responsible for something happening to the boys. He adored them, he thought miserably, loved them.

Donovan hung his head. He was responsible for what had happened at the inn. It would go up for sale now, and he and Judge Sheldon would buy it. They would be partners after all. It was what he'd wanted all along, but he felt no thrill at the turn of events. He couldn't celebrate a success that cost someone else the life they wanted. Donovan rested his forearms on the railing and stared over the acres of meadows and overgrown woodland his family owned. At a kudzu-covered tree line in the distance sat the newly renovated family guesthouse. It looked homey, cozy and inviting. Donovan knew it was generous of his parents to share the property with him. He had his own space, and he didn't have to be far from family. He was blessed, he knew, but for some insane reason, he'd begun to think of the inn as his home.

A broad arm of sunshine fanned through the trees and lit up the roof of the guesthouse. What a perfect place to start over, he thought, but he'd never be able to appreciate it if he was lonely. The thought of not having Lindsey and the boys around him filled him with a deep, dark sadness inside where Ryan's memories were etched.

Chapter Fourteen

A week passed before Claire insisted Lindsey take a break from packing and go to the library. Even though they'd grown too big, she loaded the boys into the stroller to make it easier to keep up with them. They cheered giddily, ready to escape the confines of the cottage. Rolling down the sidewalk, they passed the flagpole, the market, the café and Diane's shop, ambling through town for what Lindsey realized would probably be the last time. Soon, she'd leave for Texas to stay with her parents for a long visit and celebrate the twins' birthday away from their friend, Emily. She hoped to find a small apartment and return to her old job, if they'd have her.

As she passed the founder's museum, Lindsey stopped to read the update on the playground. The ribbon-cutting ceremony was less than a couple weeks away, and the news made her heart sink. They'd watched it come to life, but the boys would never be able to play there. "Mom!" shouted Leo, stabbing his finger in excitement toward the swings. Lindsey wheeled the stroller back around and continued to the library before there was a mutiny. "It's not ready yet, honey," she told him. The only thing lacking at this point was spreading the mulch, piled like a mountain, but there was no use in trying to explain it to two little boys.

"Play," echoed Archer.

"Let's go find Emily," Lindsey suggested. She hurried the last block to the gleaming brick warehouse that was the library and ducked inside, leaving the stroller in the lobby area.

"Boys!" called Emily in a commanding voice from across the room, and her mother shushed her. Lindsey chuckled as Leo and Archer darted off to join their friend. The children made their way to the reading corner while Lindsey silenced her phone and hurried to catch up. Claire gave her a warm hug. "Thanks for coming. Emily wanted to see them before naptime."

"They could use a break," admitted Lindsey.

"When are you heading out?"

"This weekend, I think."

"I'm going to miss you," Claire sighed, "and the help with Emily, too."

"You helped me more than I did you," Lindsey chided her.

"Who's keeping score?" Claire shrugged. "Besides, a plate of your cookies far exceeds an hour of watching three littles play together. I owe you."

Her kindness lifted Lindsey's spirits. "When Daphne gets settled, we'll visit around the holidays, maybe."

"You better." Claire looped her arm through hers and led Lindsey to the chairs set out for parents.

Lindsey couldn't help but feel Donovan's absence. "I thought Emily's favorite babysitter would be here today." A part of her was relieved, but another part was disappointed. She missed him, but the flood at the inn had finally turned the tide of their relationship, and it was time to move on. He'd won. She had to dig deep and find the courage to start over again and let go of what she'd been refusing to accept—that she cared about him. She had to put all of her dreams on hold—including him—not that she'd allowed herself to dream about him too much.

"He was here," Claire said. "He may still be here somewhere."

Lindsey looked around with burning apprehension, hoping Donovan hadn't stayed. He should be up to his ears in permits and paperwork by now. The librarian called the children together and showed them the storybook for the day. Leo and Archer crawled forward on their knees in anticipation. Claire poked Lindsey in the ribs with her elbow. "It's your turn."

"To what?"

"Go look at books. I checked some out last time."

Lindsey looked around, tempted. "I'm leaving and don't have time to read right now. You go ahead."

"You need a break," Claire insisted. "Go browse. I got this." She motioned toward the children, and with a sigh of gratitude, Lindsey thanked her and headed for the nonfiction aisle to look at cookbooks. She picked up her favorite Southern author and thumbed through the pages of the casserole section.

"I thought I'd find you here. You always

have a cookbook from the library with your book club read."

Lindsey lowered the book in surprise. She hadn't expected to find Donovan in the cooking aisle.

Seeing him again, and at such close quarters, set her heart racing. "Claire said you were around here somewhere."

Donovan gave her a guilty smile. "I wanted to talk to you. I came by the inn yesterday, but there was only a work crew there."

"I took the boys to the café," Claire explained. She turned the cookbook over and ran her fingers down the spine. "The kitchen's still a mess, and it was just easier to feed the boys that way."

"We missed you Sunday."

"I hope your mother wasn't too upset."

Donovan gave a curt nod. "We understand, but we still wished you could have come."

Lindsey's chest flooded with a quiet, fragile pleasure. How long had it been since she'd been missed? He took a step forward to close the space between them, and her heart took a swan dive. She hadn't been able to quit thinking about him. It hurt, but she needed to stay focused on what she needed to do next. "How's the charity coming together?" She tried not to sound resentful. "I guess you'll get a good deal."

"I've spoken to the bank," Donovan admitted, "and I have some ideas."

"I'm sure you do," she said with a tight smile.

He started to say more but seemed to think better of it. Lindsey appreciated it. As much as she loved him, she really didn't want to hear the details. A thought rattled her bones. Did she love him? Her throat knotted. "I should get back to the boys," she choked so he didn't know her knees felt like jelly. Lindsey lurched away.

"Wait," Donovan whispered, and his hoarse tone made her heady. He reached out and put a hand on her arm. "I was thinking—"

Lindsey sucked in a breath. This couldn't happen. She had no job, no home for her twins, and she had to go. "Don't," she whispered, and backed away. "I'm sorry, Donovan, I—I can't do this." She felt her resolve threaten to crumble. "I'm leaving." His eyes clouded with disappointment. "Daphne is going to be in Albany for a while, and I'm moving back to Texas to stay with my parents." Lindsey put on her best cheerful voice. "I might get my old job back. I have an interview in two weeks."

"That's…great." Donovan looked confused. "But I thought Kudzu Creek was your home now."

"I didn't make any plans for leaving," Lindsey admitted. "I believed the inn would make it." She stared past him at the nonfiction shelves along the back wall. "So I'm going to stay with my parents until I get back on my feet, and then I'll get my own place close by where they live."

"But you hate office work. You like to bake."

"I'll find something part-time in the evenings," she replied.

"Two jobs?"

"My parents will help with the boys. It'll be a little easier now that they're not toddlers." Lindsey stiffened her spine to make herself strong. She'd done it before, and she'd do it again. Maybe someday Donovan would be impressed, proud even, that she'd ticked off her goals, too.

He looked back toward the children surrounding the librarian. Leo and Archer were mesmerized by whatever she was reading. "That's good news, Lindsey," he said, his hands falling to his sides. "I'd assumed you could find something here, but I'm glad you worked something out."

"Me, too, and congratulations on your charity."

Donovan studied her, eyes swarming with messages and other thoughts she told herself might be too painful to hear. She scrunched her nose. "I better get back to the boys," she squeaked. "We'll stop by and see your mother before we leave."

Donovan stared at her quietly, like he wanted to say more, but she fled. She didn't spot him again after Storytime and assumed he'd gone out the library's back door by the reference books so that he didn't have to see her.

Donovan had no appetite the rest of the week and only felt worse when the weekend came. Nothing had gone as planned. He'd called Daphne twice about the inn, but she hadn't called him back. He texted Lindsey and offered to watch the boys while she finished packing, but she never responded. She was breaking ties, he knew it, distracted by her situation and the things she needed to do. Survival mode. Walls up. Windows locked. He exhaled and forced himself to go to church, hoping she would be there, which she was, but afterward her book club friends gathered around to wish her well, and she met his eyes only once when she promised Vi she'd come over to say goodbye. He'd given her a tight, faint smile, but she'd looked away. She'd made it absolutely clear. She'd shut the door on any possibility of a future together.

He drove back discouraged and wondered if he should be there when she came by to visit his mother. The quiet guesthouse was lonely, and the possibility of her bringing the twins over made him hurry home early from the office Monday and Tuesday. On Wednesday, he was finally rewarded for hanging out in the living room with his dad watching the news every night. The doorbell chimed, and Vi hurried to answer it. There was a ripple of excitement in the air as two small boys came skipping into the room.

"Uncle Don!" cried Leo.

"I'm going bye-bye," Archer informed him seriously.

Donovan crouched down and gave them both a hug. Lindsey stayed at the door speaking in low tones to his mother. "We can't stay long," he heard her apologize. "We have errands to run before we head out Friday."

"Well, come in and have some treats," Vi insisted. She shot Donovan a look as she hurried to the kitchen. His moping all week had not gone unnoticed. Donovan put a boy on each hip and carried them to the kitchen. Lindsey followed.

"Are you about packed up?" he asked, straining to make conversation.

"Yes," she assured him, not meeting his gaze. She leaned against the counter while his mother set cupcakes there. Leo clapped his hands with glee.

"Everything's unlocked upstairs for showings or whatever."

"I'm not sure there will be showings," he began. He wanted to tell her his offer had been accepted but knew now was not the time.

"Aunt Daphne will be back next weekend from Albany," Lindsey continued in a stiff tone, cutting him off. She didn't want to talk about it, and he didn't want to press the issue. "She's going to look at a few houses in town. Something cozy."

"That sounds nice," Donovan replied although he knew his tone said otherwise. "There's a lot of real estate available in the county," he hinted. "In fact, the guesthouse out back here could be available."

Lindsey shot him a look of surprise. "Don't you live there?"

It'd been in the back of his mind for days, and Donovan realized what he wanted more than the inn. He glanced at his mother, and she gave him a subtle nod of approval. "I was thinking of moving back in here for a while," Donovan announced. "You could stay there if you want."

"For as long as you need," Vi inserted.

"Oh, but I couldn't," Lindsey mumbled, studying the boys as they crammed the choc-olate-frosted cupcakes into their mouths. "I've put enough people out."

"What if Daphne needs you again?" Dono-van knew he sounded desperate. His mother shot him a glance as she turned to the sink to rinse off her hands.

"She's ready to retire," said Lindsey. "Be-sides, my parents live near the city and there's lots for the boys to do."

Donovan was out of arguments. "Good schools, too, I bet."

"Yes, and our church family." Lindsey reached over to brush her fingers through the back of Archer's hair.

"I'm glad you worked it out." Donovan wanted to grasp her hand when she finally met his eyes, but he couldn't find the cour-age under her uneasy gaze. Vi waved a large plastic storage bag. "For extras on the road when you leave."

"That's kind of you." Lindsey smiled. "Thank you, Vi."

"I bet they're not as good as yours, but I did my best."

"I'm sure they are. Say thank you," Lindsey instructed the boys. Their eyes lit up and Vi gave them each a tight hug. She turned to Lindsey next.

"You take care and call us if you need anything."

Lindsey continued to smile, but it looked pasted on, becoming even stiffer when Donovan blurted, "I'll walk you out." This was his last chance. He'd already tried to say what he needed to at the library, but that hadn't worked…

After saying goodbye to his parents, Lindsey walked back to the minivan. She opened the sliding door and deposited Archer inside while Leo wiggled down her leg. Donovan picked him up. "It's time to buckle in," he admonished. He squeezed in beside Lindsey, their shoulders touching, and gave Leo a gentle push toward the other side of the van. Just feeling her beside him made Donovan wanted to pull her into his arms and hold her until the sun went down.

She stepped back and turned to face him as if she dreaded the moment, and it punched him in the gut. Donovan took a chance to reach for her hand and found it trembling. Her fingers curled around his. "I'm going to miss you, Lindsey. I hate to see you go." His voice sounded hoarse.

Her eyes misted over, and he realized she did care. "Thank you for everything you've done."

"I wish I could have done more," he replied.

She gave a casual shrug as if the disastrous chain of events was nothing. "We gave it our best shot. Aunt Daphne and I, I mean." Her cheeks reddened. "I know the inn is in good hands," she said. "Congratulations."

"I'm not sure I want it," he confided. He lowered his voice and squeezed her hand trying hard not to beg her to stay, "I'd rather you have it."

"Really? After all your goals and research?" She gave a sad smile. "It doesn't seem like it's God's plan for me. He has the final say, you know, no matter what we want."

He cringed. Perhaps having her stay would

just prolong the inevitable. Without asking, he pulled her into his arms. He realized she knew how much he cared for her and wondered why he'd waited so long to do anything about it.

"Donovan," she murmured. Her palms found his shoulders and pushed him slightly away. "Daphne will be fine. I'll be fine, and I'll look forward to catching up. Okay?"

Donovan nodded. This was it. She was leaving and taking the boys with her. "Okay," he whispered. He dropped his hands and stepped back. No matter how much it hurt, he had to let her go. They both had dreams to chase, dreams she wanted more than he did his.

Lindsey reached around for a bag on the passenger seat and pulled out his trophy. "You left this at the inn. I thought I'd bring it back over to you." She smiled tearfully. "I hope things go well," she choked, "with Ryan's House. I know he'd be proud of you—forgive you—whatever you need." Her eyes welled up with tears. "You don't have anything to prove to anyone anymore, Donovan." A teardrop slid down her cheek, and she wiped it away with a look of mirth. "But maybe a little less planning and a little more living would be good for you."

Donovan made himself chuckle in agreement. "You're right. You'll be a great chef someday."

She gave him a small wave. "I'll message you when we get settled."

"Please do."

With that, Lindsey rounded the front of the van, climbed in and drove back toward town. Leo waved wildly from the side window as they pulled away, and after watching them disappear with a smile frozen on his face, Donovan stalked off around the house and started across the field toward the guest quarters with his eyes smarting. A lump grew in his throat that he could not swallow down. He stared hard into the sun until it blinded him, and for the first time since his best friend's funeral, a few tears fell.

"Donovan!"

He sucked in a quiet sob at his mother's voice. Looking down on him from the deck, she motioned for him to come back to the house. With a haggard sigh, he wiped his eyes and returned to the backyard, then jogged up the steep stairs to the second-story porch.

"Did you talk to her any more about the guesthouse?"

"She said no," he croaked. He dropped down into a lounge chair, unable to bear his mother's sympathetic expression.

"That was a good idea. I wish I'd thought of it. Donovan?"

He slid his gaze sideways.

"It's not just the twins, is it? You're in love with her."

"Yes, I figured that out the day we went to the creek."

"What happened? Oh, I know. You kissed her, didn't you?"

Donovan's cheeks caught fire. "Mom!"

"Have you told her that you love her?"

"Not exactly."

"Why not?" complained Vi.

He gave a tight, rebellious shrug. "She already has her little family."

"Don."

His mother's voice filled him with remorse. He sighed. "She has her own dreams. She doesn't want any help, because she doesn't trust anyone with them." He gave her a meaningful look. "Especially lawyers."

Vi gave a soft snort. "It's not your fault the inn went into foreclosure." She gazed out over the yard just barely keeping the distant mounds of kudzu at bay. "Are you going to simply give up because she's as scared as you are?"

Donovan chewed the inside of his cheek.

"Honey, you've never been afraid to take a risk and work hard, but I know you'll never be happy if you don't give up what you *think* you want and go after love instead. Your life's joy will never be found on a plaque or in a magazine. You may even lose, but if you win…"

Donovan shut his eyes in a long, slow blink. "Please don't give me the grandbaby talk right now."

"I'd automatically have two," Vi teased. "And you could live in the guesthouse or even the cottage behind the Azalea Inn. It would be fun!"

"It's just a dream, Mom," Donovan muttered. He gazed out over the backyard. The truth was the inn was too beautiful to be turned into a halfway house. It was a home, and it needed a family.

Chapter Fifteen

"Just where do you think you're going?"

Lindsey froze at the sound of the familiar, teasing voice. She turned from cramming a snack bag into the tightly packed van. "Aunt Daphne! What are you doing back early?"

Aunt Daphne closed the distance between them, her pinstriped overalls a welcome sight. She wrapped Lindsey in a hug. "I drove back this morning. We have a lot to do."

Lindsey glanced back at the house she'd just secured. "I'm afraid I was just pulling out. We told everyone goodbye yesterday and the day before."

"You're not staying for the playground's grand opening?"

"They're doing the ribbon-cutting ceremony tomorrow," Lindsey reminded her. "I wanted to be on the road by then so we could be with Mom and Dad on Sunday."

Aunt Daphne looked oddly content. "Are you all right?" wondered Lindsey. "The cleanup crew finished, so the inn is ready for repairs."

"Yes, and I plan to oversee them while looking for a little bungalow." Aunt Daphne released Lindsey and walked over to Leo and bussed his cheek.

"Dappy!" cried both twins from their car seats in delight.

"I missed you guys more than I thought I would," she admitted. She turned to Lindsey. "In fact, I think a little twin time every day is good for me. What do you say?"

"Oh no," said Lindsey. "I couldn't possibly ask you to take us in again."

"Actually, I was thinking about the cottage."

Lindsey crinkled her brow. "I have to find a job, and with the inn shut down…"

"What do you mean *shut down*?" Aunt Daphne grinned.

"I don't understand. Haven't they started foreclosure?"

"You haven't heard from Donovan?"

"Not today." Lindsey's face flushed, and to

her horror, her eyes teared. "I told him good-bye earlier this week."

"Now, why would you do that when you care about him so much?" Aunt Daphne chided her.

Lindsey began to cry. "I do. I know it's obvious, but I have nowhere else to go. I got my old job back, and he's busy with his plans, and I need to move on, or I'm never going to have my own restaurant. It turns out Kudzu Creek isn't right for me."

"I have something better for you, and if you love Donovan as much as I think you do, you don't need to leave Kudzu Creek to find another home. You make one. Here. And follow your heart instead of your fears."

Lindsey stared in surprise. Aunt Daphne threw an arm around her shoulders and spun her around to face the inn. "The Azalea Inn has a second owner—a co-owner, if you will—and we need a manager to run the place and prepare a hot breakfast every morning."

Lindsey looked at her as if she was delirious. "What are you talking about? Who?"

"Donovan Ainsworth, of course. He offered to pay our outstanding debt if I'd split ownership with him and donate the cottage's living space for his new charity."

"Ryan's House?" Lindsey's jaw went numb.

"Ryan's House will be a cottage, and the nonprofit address will be a P.O. box," explained Aunt Daphne.

Donovan had given up using the inn for his charity? Lindsey's mind spun. But he'd had it all worked out, even had Judge Sheldon on board. Had he done it all for Aunt Daphne… or for her?

"You can stay in the cottage for now, until you and the boys can move back inside the inn. It'd help if you could oversee the reno for me, to be honest," hinted Aunt Daphne.

"But what about the twins?"

"You let me worry about that. I've decided to become a babysitter instead of an entrepreneur. That's if you'll take over as manager."

"Of course I will!" Lindsey exclaimed.

"Until we get the old girl back on her feet? Then you can return to the kitchen."

"That sounds like a dream come true!"

"I'm even considering letting Isaac come back," announced Aunt Daphne. "Maybe you could train him to run things, like an assistant manager."

"I'm sure I could!" blurted Lindsey. Tears erupted without warning and streamed from the corners of her eyes. "Did you hear that, boys? We get to stay at the Azalea Inn."

Leo leaned from his car seat with a quizzical stare. "Where's *Emiwee*?"

Lindsey laughed, her heart soaring like an untethered bird. God's plan was to see her dreams come true after all, if not in the way she'd pictured. She would manage a little, cook a little and love her boys a lot. She would be forever grateful to the lawyer who treated the twins like his own. "We can see Emily tomorrow. And I know just the place for a playdate!"

Donovan parked across the street from the museum. It was strange using a car to get around again, but the guesthouse was too far out in the country to walk to the playground's grand opening. His feet felt like lead as he dragged himself from the car, but Bradley had called to make sure he went through with his promise to Emily to show up. Besides that, his law office had donated money to fund equipment, too, and it was only right Donovan be there with the other sponsors. Not that he wanted any recognition—or needed it—but it was too late. He'd changed, yes, and because of a woman who'd taken her life back to Texas. Lindsey had touched him, and he was a better person in ways he knew Ryan would be proud of, even if he had a long road ahead getting over a broken heart. Donovan told himself things ending with Lindsey were better this way. If they'd made anything official or there'd been a serious commitment between them, it would have made things awkward around town, and overshadowed Ryan's House.

Throngs of people mingled around lemonade and cotton candy stands as a loud whoop went up. Clapping and cheering filled the air. Donovan assumed Judge Sheldon had cut the ribbon to the playground, and he'd missed it. He took a deep breath and walked around the corner of the museum. Children swarmed the grounds, and he forced himself not to search for Leo and Archer. They would have loved playing on the equipment. Seeing Ms. Olivia, Donovan made a beeline for the wise, older woman. She was perched in a lawn chair wearing a floppy hat and enormous sunglasses. "You came out to see the new playground." Donovan didn't hide his admiration.

She crooked a finger at him. "Of course I did. I went to this museum when it was a school. Plus, I'm on the Chamber of Commerce board," she reminded him.

Donovan nodded, not bothering to mention her honorary status on the board.

"It's about time we had a park where children can gather," Ms. Olivia continued. She swung her drooping neck over her shoulder. "Look! There's Laurel. She's the new Chamber president, you know."

"Yes, and still presiding over the historical-preservation committee. You stay out of the sun if you can, Ms. Olivia." Donovan squeezed her wizened hand and continued wading through the children scurrying back and forth. Green and yellow paint made the climbing towers, swings and slides stand out. Standing nearby, Judge Sheldon was surrounded by friends and coworkers. Donovan pushed through the crowd and offered his hand. "Congratulations."

"Thank you." The judge beamed.

"I know this was one of your projects with the Chamber."

"It's going to be a great place for families to gather," Judge Sheldon said. Donovan spied a small walking path with a few benches circling the playground. It looked perfect for joggers and strollers. "I guess you've found your gathering place, too. You always said you needed some place to relax beside Southern Fried Kudzu."

"That I did," cried the judge.

"It's special." Donovan cleared his throat to tackle the proverbial elephant in the room. "Thank you for understanding about the inn. It just didn't feel right turning it over to a charity—even mine."

The judge nodded solemnly. "I hate missing out on owning a piece of that beautiful house, but I'm happy to be on the board if you still need me."

"Are you?"

The judge made a wry face. "It's the least I can do."

Donovan smiled as relief washed over him. At least he hadn't burned any bridges. His stomach sank when he realized he'd failed to build the one he wanted most. He scanned the crowd.

"There really is no greater achievement in the world than raising your kids right," said Judge Sheldon to a parent beside them. Donovan knew he had no idea how the words stung. He'd always wanted a family, and when the time came, he'd let them slip through his fingers. He tried not to let his throat clog up with emotion and exhaled with relief when he saw Bradley and Claire. He wandered over to cheer himself up.

Ryan's House would happen. The inn was saved. Judge Sheldon wasn't angry, and Daphne would be back soon. After he finally got a hold of her and presented his plan, she'd said she needed a break and would get back to him about the details later, but the deal was done. He'd pay her debts, and they'd sign off on the paperwork making him part owner of the Azalea Inn. Now he just needed to help her find a new manager—one that could at least bake a pan of muffins. He wilted a little inside and reminded himself to put on a professional, happy face. No one needed to know he was devastated because he'd never have the relationship with Lindsey and the twins that he ached for more than any other achievement. The sun burned down on the top of his head, and he let it work on incinerating his heart, too.

"They did a great job." Bradley smiled as Donovan approached. His cousin pointed at Emily on the top of a slide, looking around the park like it was her kingdom.

"Yes, it's going to be a great addition to town."

"Like the newly rescued inn?" Bradley teased.

Donovan shrugged. "I guess. It's getting a new paint job. It may look a little different."

"I think white will be lovely," chimed in Claire. "It's fresh and bright and new." She met Donovan's stare and inclined her head. "You've done an amazing, honorable thing helping Daphne out. Are you doing okay?"

"Fine."

"Have you talked to Lindsey yet?"

"Not since she left," he replied in a terse tone. He wanted to forget about her, to erase everything from his brain like it was a hard drive, but he knew that wouldn't happen. He'd just made peace with Ryan, so why had God handed someone else to haunt him?

"How do things look for the charity?"

"We're almost up and running," Donovan answered, grateful for the change of subject. "I had Isaac fill out an application today, but it's just for the files. He'll move into the cottage in a few weeks and keep an eye on things until the repairs are done."

"So he's going to manage it?" Bradley asked.

"Until Daphne can get someone full time. She said she'd start asking around, but once things are staffed, she's going to take a back seat. She's retiring."

"That sounds great. I think maybe she was ready for this," said Claire. "We're so proud of you, Donovan," she added and squeezed his arm. "Ryan would be, too." Emily shouted for her, and Claire moved off.

"So, are you satisfied now?" Bradley wondered with concern. "You have your charity for Ryan. You even saved the inn."

"I think I can finally let him rest in peace." Donovan slid his hands into his pockets and rocked on his feet, watching children around him play without a care in the world.

"I hope you'll get some rest, too," said his cousin, "because I think you still have some things left to tackle."

"What do you mean?"

"There's more to resolve than just Ryan's House," Bradley observed.

"What?"

"Forgiving yourself?"

Donovan felt his defenses go up.

"You're a pretty determined guy," continued Bradley in a reserved tone. "I've never seen you waste a minute on anything you didn't think would work out. And since you had so much guilt, I always figured it was something more than just not being there for him, like why you didn't feel like you could."

Donovan passed a hand over his brow. The playground equipment would be too hot to play on soon. He knew the why. He didn't like failures. He didn't want to invest any of himself into something that would be left dangling unfinished over the sides of his goal sheet. "You're right," he blurted. "I don't fight hard if I don't think I can win. In fact, I don't fight at all unless I'm going to get something out of it. It's wrong, and it's selfish." He bit his bottom lip hard and winced. Bradley patted him on the shoulder as if to tell him to take it easy.

"Ryan made choices I didn't like so I wrote him off." Donovan cringed. "I know opening a halfway house isn't going to bring him back, but I need to make sure kids like him know they're worth it."

Bradley shuffled his feet in the mulch. "That can't be all that's bothering you."

"Of course not," Donovan huffed. "I helped Daphne save the inn, but Sheldon probably won't talk about me becoming a judge ever again—at least not for a long time."

"I think he understands. What about that county property?"

Donovan shook his head. "I waited too long. It's gone." He swallowed down the bitterness and said under his breath with an excruciating sigh, "Like Lindsey." Children were all over the playground except Leo and Archer he observed with despair.

"Was she worth fighting for?"

"I tried, but not hard enough. I didn't risk everything, and I should have."

"What made you hesitate?"

"Losing. She made it clear she was ready to go home," Donovan said. "She's so independent. Stubborn. She has too much pride to let people help her and acts like her situation is her own fault." He groaned. "It's not like we looked good on paper, anyway, so I just...gave up."

"Not good on paper? That's the old you talking again," Bradley pointed out with irritation.

"If I thought I had a chance, I—"

"Taking chances is almost always worth it," Bradley said firmly. "The right ones. You wanted a guarantee. You didn't want another failed relationship on your record."

Donovan stared at his cousin. "Kind of harsh, coming from you, isn't it?"

"You know my story," Bradley shrugged.

"How can I ever regret what I had with Emily's mother? It didn't work out, but it doesn't mean I failed. I moved on, and in the long run, I was blessed."

"I don't want to move on," grunted Donovan. The heat was getting to him. "I should tell Emily goodbye. Uncle Don has done his duty for today."

Bradley's gaze drifted across the crowd. "Why don't you do that," he said in a strange voice. "Tell Emily goodbye, and then go for it this time, instead of making a checklist and weighing your options."

Donovan followed his cousin's gaze in confusion, and his heart plummeted to his shoes. Lindsey, Archer and Leo were standing in a small circle around the slide with Claire. He blinked to make sure he wasn't hallucinating. Lindsey's hair was up in a ponytail. It made her look slightly taller and as beautiful as ever. She was home!

The twins wiggled past her while she was chatting and started up the tall ladder to the slide. Donovan's eyes widened. He watched Leo scramble up like a mountain goat. With a gasp, Donovan sprinted across the playground and reached the slide just as Leo came swooping down out of control. Donovan caught him just as he let out a bellowing wail that made all heads turn their direction. He scooped him up in his arms, and Leo looked up in surprise, suddenly healed. "Uncle Don," he cried, then touched his forehead gingerly.

Donovan brought him to his chest and held him tight. "Are you okay, buddy?"

"I'm okay," Leo chirped, but he laid his head on Donovan's shoulder like he felt a little unsure.

"Leo!"

Donovan's heart cartwheeled again, and he turned to face the boy's mother. Lindsey took a step back and put a hand to her heart. "Donovan!"

Leo twisted around and looked. "It's fine, Mom."

A small laugh blurted from Lindsey's lips. "Okay."

"He's learned from the best. He's fine," Donovan teased. *I'm not,* he thought. *But you and the boys will be.*

Leo wiggled, and Donovan released him to the ground. "Don't go down that slide again, Leo. It's too big. Try that one." He pointed toward the option for small children. Leo frowned.

"Leo, why don't you look in the playhouse?"

Lindsey suggested. She watched him scamper off and turned to Donovan. "I didn't think we'd see you here." Another child whizzed between them, and Donovan forced a nervous chuckle.

"Judge Sheldon was doing the ribbon cutting, and—" He realized his heart was pounding so hard it made his voice tremble. He flushed with chagrin. "I wasn't expecting you here. You're..." He lowered his brows. "Daphne said..."

"She's back from Albany."

"I thought you left yesterday."

"She surprised me." Lindsey gave a light laugh, and he thought she sounded nervous. Her eyes flitted back and forth between the museum and his gaze—searching deeply, he thought. She reached for his hand, and Donovan's heart leaped. "She told me about the inn, Donovan. What you did."

"You know?"

"Yes, I know."

Donovan's chest tightened. "And you stayed?" He looked around the playground. "For the ribbon cutting?"

Lindsey laughed. "No. I mean, yes, I didn't want to miss it. But there's been a change of—" she looked at him and beamed "—plans."

"What plans?"

"Daphne offered me the management job. I'll be able to cook a little, too, but for now, just breakfasts."

The weight of the world seemed to fly off Donovan's shoulders. His chest. His heart. "Management? You're staying for good?"

"Yes," Lindsey informed him. She sent him a meaningful look that made him burn from head to toe in a happy thrill that had nothing to do with the sunny day.

"But what about the twins?"

"I was able to find a very good childcare provider. Aunt Daphne's going to try out a new career."

Donovan glanced back at Claire and flushed when he found her and Bradley watching. Lindsey followed his gaze. "I'm still going to Texas to visit in a few days, but the boys and I are coming back home."

"Home?"

Lindsey's eyes shimmered with tears. "This is home. I think I've always known it. " She squeezed Donovan's hand, and he wrapped his fingers around hers. "This feels right," she repeated.

. "Lindsey," he exclaimed, heart galloping, "you will never be wanted or needed anywhere more than you are here." Donovan pulled her hand to his chest, and the passion in her eyes made him dare to reach out and caress her cheek. "And there is nothing I wouldn't do to make you feel at home."

A faint smile pulled at the corner of Lindsey's mouth. Donovan gently pulled her to him and met her halfway. A smile bloomed across her face, and her cheeks glowed as pink as the azaleas at the inn just as he closed his eyes and sealed his words with a kiss.

Epilogue

The front porch light of the Azalea Inn shone in the late September humidity for any guests who'd stayed out after Kudzu Creek's shops had closed for the night. Lindsey shut the door to the office, clicked off the lamp on the front desk, then returned to the dining room with a glance at the old grandfather clock, which assured her the twins would be asleep by now.

Laughter erupted around the table in the middle of the room as she reached to pull out her chair. Beside it, her husband jumped to his feet to help. "Sit. There hasn't been a peep upstairs since I came down, Donovan promised."

Lindsey slipped into her seat, and beside her, Claire leaned into her shoulder. "We've finished dessert," she whispered in a conspiratorial tone, then motioned toward Donovan. Lindsey folded her hands across her stomach and scanned the table. Bradley, Aunt Daphne and Judge Sheldon were discussing the sheriff's election in enthusiastic tones. The judge's wife and Diane were comparing daily caloric intakes while Vi and Harold Ainsworth taste-tested each other's apple cobbler. Scooted back from the table, Mac and Isaac watched something on Isaac's tablet and laughed again. Lindsey gave Claire a nod, and her best friend clinked her fork against her glass. "Attention!" she called. When everyone quieted, she said with great solemnity, "Lindsey has an announcement."

Lindsey felt Donovan's inquisitive gaze. His leg pressed against hers, and she reached down to pat him with affection. Her heart swelled with love for the man who'd given her more than she'd dared to dream. "I have a special announcement to make."

Judge Sheldon's brows furrowed. "What's the news? A new home for Ryan's House?"

"The charity is doing well," cut in Donovan, shooting Lindsey a questioning look. "But we're staying with the cottage for now." He gave Isaac a nod, and the young man beamed back.

"Then, what is it?" Something like excitement flickered in Vi's eyes, and Lindsey knew her mother-in-law suspected more than she was letting on.

"It's about the head count at the inn," said Lindsey carefully. Vi sucked in a gasp.

"The guest list?" Donovan was confused now, and Claire giggled.

Lindsey looked around the table at the people who'd become her friends and family just as the Azalea Inn had become her home. "We have a new guest on the way." She smiled and turned to Donovan. "In a little less than eight months." Lindsey put her hand on her stomach for emphasis. For a split second, Donovan's brows teetered over his hazel eyes in consideration, but then he sat back in his chair, breathless.

Vi and Diane jumped to their feet simultaneously and cheered while everyone clapped. Donovan pulled Lindsey into a tight embrace and buried his face in her neck. His cedar scent tickled her nose, and she burrowed her forehead into his dark curls. "You're sure?" his thick voice whispered in her ear.

"I'm sure," she replied softly. She looked back up at her friends, who were glowing with happiness for her and her little family.

"And you'll all be happy to know that today I received official word that it's just one. Not twins."

Judge Sheldon hooted. Lindsey felt Donovan relax in her arms and burst into laughter. "You're off the hook," she teased. "There is no double trouble on the way for the county's newest district attorney."

Her husband planted a firm kiss on her cheek, gave her an intimate wink, and turned back to their friends. "Three kids, two twins and a chef at my side." He smiled. "I guess I have nothing left to shoot for."

"Then you can check everything off your lists and throw them away," teased Bradley. Their friends burst into cheers, and this time, Donovan joined them with his greatest achievement at his side.

* * * * *

Dear Reader,

I hope you enjoyed *A Home for the Twins*, my second story in Kudzu Creek, where people look out for their neighbors and believe family is a gift from God. Writing Donovan and Lindsey's story was a joy. As a sister to four brothers and a mother of four sons, I am also now Grandma Dee Dee to a matching set of beautiful little boys who inspired the sweetness and mischief in this romance.

Having faith in your dreams is hard; forging ahead when you fail is scary. We can't control others' choices, but we can love them through it, and if their actions affect us negatively, we can go forward with faith, even if that means being vulnerable all over again.

Thanks for reading my book. I hope you found love, inspiration, and the courage to live life the way God prompts you to live it. Thank you to my patient, loving family and friends, review team, and the editors and staff at Harlequin for supporting me on my writing journey.

Much love,
Danielle Thorne.